Cruz didn't move. 3·00

He sat right there while Rory smooched little Javier and ruffled his hair, and when she was done kissing him, Cruz leaned in and kissed the boy, too. They said one last good-night, then he followed her out, into the hall. Before they were halfway down the stairs, she paused and looked back. "You surprised me in there."

"Because I knew prayers?"

"Not that." She stayed on the second step and faced him. "You kissed them good-night."

"I believe that's customary with small children, isn't it?"

"It is, but you don't have small children, do you?"

He shook his head.

"And I don't expect you do a lot of babysitting in Manhattan."

"No, again."

She almost spoke again, then stopped herself. "I just thought it was nice, that's all. You made them smile."

She started back down the stairs to rejoin the others. Five little words made her stop again.

"That's why I did it."

She turned and looked up, and when she did, her heart did that shuffle-step dance once more.

Multipublished, bestselling author **Ruth Logan Herne** loves God, her country, her family, dogs, chocolate and coffee! Married to a very patient man, she lives in an old farmhouse in upstate New York and thinks possums should leave the cat food alone and snakes should always live outside. There are no exceptions to either rule! Visit Ruthy at ruthloganherne.com.

Books by Ruth Logan Herne

Love Inspired

Grace Haven

An Unexpected Groom
Her Unexpected Family
Their Surprise Daddy

Kirkwood Lake

The Lawman's Second Chance
Falling for the Lawman
The Lawman's Holiday Wish
Loving the Lawman
Her Holiday Family
Healing the Lawman's Heart

Men of Allegany County

Small-Town Hearts
Mended Hearts
Yuletide Hearts
A Family to Cherish
His Mistletoe Family

Visit the Author Profile page at Harlequin.com for more titles.

Their Surprise Daddy

Ruth Logan Herne

If you purchased this book without a cover you should be aware
that this book is stolen property. It was reported as "unsold and
destroyed" to the publisher, and neither the author nor the
publisher has received any payment for this "stripped book."

Recycling programs
for this product may
not exist in your area.

LOVE INSPIRED BOOKS

ISBN-13: 978-0-373-62275-7

Their Surprise Daddy

Copyright © 2017 by Ruth M. Blodgett

All rights reserved. Except for use in any review, the reproduction
or utilization of this work in whole or in part in any form by any
electronic, mechanical or other means, now known or hereinafter
invented, including xerography, photocopying and recording, or in
any information storage or retrieval system, is forbidden without
the written permission of the editorial office, Love Inspired Books,
195 Broadway, New York, NY 10007 U.S.A.

This is a work of fiction. Names, characters, places and incidents are
either the product of the author's imagination or are used fictitiously, and
any resemblance to actual persons, living or dead, business establishments,
events or locales is entirely coincidental.

This edition published by arrangement with Love Inspired Books.

® and TM are trademarks of Love Inspired Books, used under license.
Trademarks indicated with ® are registered in the United States Patent
and Trademark Office, the Canadian Intellectual Property Office and in
other countries.

www.Harlequin.com

Printed in U.S.A.

"And I will be a father to you,
and you shall be sons and daughters to Me,"
says the Lord Almighty.
—*2 Corinthians* 6:18

To my dear friend Mia Ross,
who has shared a delightful number of years
with me… Thank you for always being
a shining light of common sense and humor!
We are so blessed to be able to work together!

Acknowledgments

To my sons, Luke and Zach,
whose lives in Lower Manhattan help me
mold characters from all walks of life,
and to my amazing editor, Melissa Endlich,
whose keen eye helped hone the lump of coal into
a polished gem of a story! Thank you!

To show respect for our police forces across the
USA, all men in the Grace Haven series have been
given names of fallen police officers, both local
officers here in my upstate area (A. J. Sperr and
Daryl Pierson) and from the 2014 fallen-officer list
provided on the Downed Officers website.
My husband and I have friends and family
who wear the uniform with pride and grace,
and our respect for them never falters.
Cruz Maldonado was named for Deputy Sheriff
Steven LaCruz "Cruz" Thomas of California.

Huge thanks to my beautiful friends
Karen and Matt Varricchio of Canandaigua for
their help on locations, seasonal workers and life
in a Finger Lakes town. We love you guys!

Chapter One

One minute Cruz Maldonado was a sought-after Manhattan financial investor with a law degree, a force to be reckoned with on Wall Street.

The next he was the guardian for two children whose existence probably sprang from the jaws of Mexican cartels.

This couldn't be happening. And yet, it was.

Cruz frowned as he drove his pricey rental car toward the Grace Haven town hall. The long midsummer day gave him a good view of the hometown he hadn't seen in years. At some point he'd greet the mother he hadn't visited since his father's funeral, the woman who'd raised him to be just as tough and jaded as she was.

You need to come home, Cruz, Reverend Steve Gallagher had told him during the unexpected phone call that morning. *Two kids, no records, a falsified paper trail and your mother's dealing with heart disease complicated by type 2 diabetes, seriously compromising her health. It would be wrong of me to make any decisions without you.*

Cruz didn't just tamp his emotions down. He fought them into submission. For long years he hadn't heard from his mother. His phone calls went straight to voice mail. His Christmas gifts came back, unopened. By the fifth year, he'd stopped trying and worked to make himself one of New York City's toughest investment funds managers, respected in international circles, and he'd succeeded.

And now this.

He checked his watch. Whatever was going on, whatever mess his mother had gotten herself into, he had every intention of returning to the city the next morning. By afternoon he'd hand in the keys of the upscale rental car and return to his desk overlooking the Hudson. Tomorrow afternoon couldn't get here soon enough.

He parked the car and strode inside, legally and mentally prepared to put an end to the nonsense. He rounded the corner of the quaint town hall, then thrust out his arms to keep from barreling into a young woman carrying a small child. "Whoa."

"Whoa?" The little boy placed tiny hands over his mouth and giggled out loud. "He finks you're a horse, Miss Wory."

"Does he now?" The woman—the *beautiful* woman— raised her eyes to his while his grip kept her from slipping to the floor.

"No. He doesn't." Cruz held her gaze and her attention as he quickly corrected the boy's assertion. He arched his right brow, nice and slow. "He doesn't think you're a horse at all. In fact, that would be about the last thing he'd think while looking at you."

"'Cause she's not, siwwy." The child giggled again,

a happy sound, about as unfamiliar to Cruz now as it had been when he was growing up in Grace Haven. "She's my teacher!"

Cruz made sure she was steady before releasing her arms, then acknowledged the boy's statement with a frank glance of appreciation. "I lived here for eighteen years. I never had a teacher that looked like this." She had gorgeous eyes, a mix of caramel and gold that matched her long tawny hair.

She started to reply, but then the boy turned her way, plainly worried. "Huwwy, Miss Wory! Huwwy."

She hustled the child to the restrooms down the hall while Cruz entered the small courtroom marked "Judge Murdoch" on the door.

"Cruz." Reverend Steve Gallagher saw him come through the door and quickly moved forward extending his hand. "Welcome home." Steve oversaw a local church and the antiquated abbey abutting Casa Blanca, the picturesque vineyard and event center where Cruz grew up.

This wasn't home, and it hadn't really been home when he lived there, but he wasn't going to argue with the cleric. Steve Gallagher was a fine man and a great neighbor. Cruz gripped his hand. "It's good to see you, Reverend Gallagher."

"Good to see you, too, son, but we're all grown up. Steve works just fine." The reverend clasped his hand in a firm, friendly grip. He motioned to the man standing nearby. "This is Judge Murdoch. Your mother's case was brought to his attention."

As Cruz reached out to shake the other man's hand, Steve added, "Thanks for getting here so quickly."

Cruz turned his attention back to Steve. "You left

me little choice, and I'm fairly certain you knew the summons was out of left field and issued it, anyway."

"Because you and your mother haven't spoken in years." Direct and honest, two qualities Cruz had always liked about Steve.

"My father played intermediary. Once he was gone, well…" Cruz shrugged. "My mother made it plain I wasn't needed or welcome here."

"You're needed now."

Cruz *was* needed, but not in this full-of-itself, old-fashioned town. He was needed right where he'd been up until five and a half hours ago, tucked in Lower Manhattan, making more money than most men see in a lifetime. "Reverend, I—"

"Ah, Rory, perfect." The reverend smiled beyond him, as if he'd said nothing. "I'm glad you're back."

"It seems I'm not the only one being offered limited options," she told Steve. Cruz had to hand it to her. Dissing clergy wasn't a skill that got practiced much, even in Manhattan.

Steve Gallagher laughed, unaffronted. "True enough. Cruz, meet my niece, Aurora Gallagher. She's the summertime pre-K teacher here in Grace Haven. And this—" he reached out and palmed the little guy's head "—is Javier. He's the youngest of your new responsibilities."

Cruz stared from the cute kid to the minister. "Reverend Gallagher—Steve," he corrected himself. "You've got this all wrong. There's no way I can—"

"I found a toad, Reverend Steve!" A little girl sporting twin ponytails bounded through the door. Her presence hiked the room's energy level as she slid to a stop near Steve's legs.

"A lively one at that," Steve replied. The gray-green toad bounded to the floor from her tiny fingers. "Cruz." His tone changed. Softened. "This is Liliana."

The girl didn't peek up at him like her brother had done. She lifted her gaze as if excited by all life had to offer, brows raised, brown eyes sparkling, and grinned.

Elina.

The child was the absolute image of her mother, his beloved cousin, playmate and childhood best friend. Through all the turbulence of his parents' marriage, Elina had looked after him, played with him and sheltered him. He owed her. He owed her so much, and yet he'd let time and space separate them long ago, and never looked back.

He swallowed hard, facing Elina's daughter, and knew what he had to do, but hated having to do it because the last place Cruz wanted to be was in Grace Haven, New York.

"Tara, can you take the kids down the hall to see the aquarium? Cruz, you remember my daughter, Tara, don't you?"

Cruz smiled and extended a hand in greeting. "I believe you had pigtails and braces when we last met."

"An awkward stage only recently corrected," Tara replied, laughing. She shook his hand, then took the little fellow from her cousin. "I'll keep these guys busy for a few minutes while you make plans."

The only plan Cruz intended to make involved a checkbook and an escape route.

"Our church is part of the ICM," Steve told him.

Cruz had no idea what that meant. He folded his arms over his chest because just the thought of Grace

Haven made him feel defensive. The reality of being here magnified the emotion. "Which is what?"

"The International Children's Ministry is a nationally certified group that maintains legal jurisdiction for foreign children in times of crisis. We have the power to place children in foster care by approved members of the church and/or the community, along with the laws of a given locality. Dual guardianship is required in all cases."

"So you are actually authorized to place these children into care in light of my mother's health problems, despite the shaky legalities?"

"I have the legal right, and the moral obligation that goes along with it," Steve told him. He swept Cruz and the honey-haired young woman a troubled look. "I'm sure this was nothing either of you expected to be thrust into today, but if there's one thing that can be said about life, it's that things are guaranteed to change when you least expect it."

"Or when people fail to follow legal procedures with little regard to who's affected." The teacher directed a frank gaze to her uncle.

"Rosa's been ill…"

The young woman held up a hand. "I understand that better than most, but the welfare of a child should always come first. And leaving these two precious little ones in legal limbo could mean a quick ticket back to Mexico, when a fairly simple process would have at least made them American citizens. Right now I'm wishing their mother or great-aunt had taken the steps to do the right thing."

Who did she think she was?

A burr prickled beneath Cruz's collar, because no

matter how attractive this woman might be, she didn't have the right to attack his family. Even when they were wrong. "You have a law degree, miss?"

"Of course not."

"And you've spent exactly how much of your life being a Latina immigrant?"

His attempt to make her feel bad backfired. "Not being an immigrant doesn't make me the bad guy here. There are a lot of folks in the Finger Lakes area who have worked exclusively with the migrant and immigrant communities, and I happen to be one of them, so save your breath. I do have respect for the law, and as a lawyer, I'm a little surprised you take it so casually. But then, maybe things are different in the big city. Maybe breaking the laws for one's personal convenience is more common in Manhattan. You would know that better than I, of course."

Touché.

Steve grimaced. "While we can't change what's happened to put us in this predicament, we might be able to solve the problem, working together."

Working together was not going to happen. Cruz knew it, but he listened out of respect for a good man, while biting back the urge to look at his watch.

"As I was saying," Steve continued, facing his niece, "the kids know you. You've known them through your friendship with Rosa, and you've been Lily's summertime teacher for two years, and Javier's since last month. They trust you. They need you, even if the timing is less than perfect because I know you've been hard at work on your upcoming project. And while I hate messing up your plans, I really need you on board for this."

She stared up at him, then drew a deep breath, but before Cruz could shrug the whole thing off and get back in his car, the reverend nailed him with a firm look. "This doesn't let you off the hook. I'm naming you as the second guardian, Cruz. It's your family, after all. As an attorney it will be your job to make recommendations to the court about where the kids should go once all this is said and done. Your mother's compromised health adds a complicating factor to an already convoluted legal situation."

"What?" He stepped back, hands up. What was Steve thinking? Didn't their family history speak for itself? Raising children had never ranked high on the list and the children's current situation highlighted that. "I have no vested interest in this, or anything else here. I am not taking on the care or guardianship of two children, and I actually have a job over five hours away. You need to find someone else to step in if you need two guardians to fulfill the obligation. Someone local."

"We don't need a second person," the young woman said smoothly. "I am totally capable of caring for Lily and Javier myself."

"The rules require dual caretakers," the judge reminded them. "Steve and I are bound by that."

"When innocent children are caught in legal battles, someone has to put them first," Steve added. "Hence the dual guardianship." Steve turned to face Cruz more directly. "If you're *really* too busy to stay and help out for a few weeks, my only recourse is to send the children out of the area to a place where the rules will be followed." Steve held Cruz's gaze. "Just so you know, if I do that, it will crush your mother."

So now he was suddenly supposed to care about his mother?

Not gonna happen.

He turned and faced the young woman. "You don't have a husband or significant other that can sign on for the duration? Because one of us has a job to do."

She held his gaze for long, slow beats, then shifted her attention to her uncle. "We live in one of the best little towns in America." There was no stopping the guilt that crept up his spine as she went on. "I expect we've got at least one good person who will step up to the plate to oversee the children with me."

Dashing footsteps announced the children's race down the long, tiled hall.

"I win!" Javier fist-pumped the air as he slid into the room, jubilant when he spun to face his older sister.

"You did!" Lily hugged the little guy as if she hadn't deliberately slowed her pace to allow his victory. *"Es muy bien, Javi!"*

Her voice. Her words. Her encouragement, so like her mother's before her.

Cruz glanced down. Big mistake, because Lily stared up at him, a miniature of the best friend he'd ever had.

Cruz! Let's climb to the hayloft! Let's check the little goats, see if they've gotten loose! Let's go bother Ninny for a snack!

They'd grown up together, cousins by birth and friends by proximity, pestering every caretaker they ever had. Only Cruz's father had married the rich American landowner and Elina's mother...

His heart grew tight, remembering.

Elina's mother hadn't married anyone, ever. She'd

had two kids out of wedlock, Elina and Juan. Juan had been killed in a drug sting on the border nearly fifteen years ago. Elina had gone back to Mexico and...

He had no idea what happened to his old friend and cousin, because he'd never bothered to check up on her. Guilt mushroomed.

He kept his gaze on the children, hands linked, and a voice sounded from somewhere inside him, a place he thought he'd lost a long time ago. "I'll do it. I'll stand guardian for them with the teacher."

He felt her eyes on him, and he was pretty sure he was about the last person on earth she'd pick to watch over these two children for however long the legal process took. But he was equally sure he had no choice in the matter because Elina had been more than his cousin. She'd been his friend when he truly needed one. It was way past time to return the favor.

Rory Gallagher's life was one strike away from being called out at the plate by a series of bad pitches.

The filing date for the elongated grant application to help fund her dream preschool for disadvantaged kids loomed in late August. The application process also stated that the school site would be upgraded to meet state standards, and she needed to find this site in an accessible part of a town where real estate sold quicker than water flowing from a tap. On top of that, the popularity of Grace Haven as a place to live, work, play and pray had pushed property values through the roof, making potential sites scarce.

Fortunately, her summer Universal Pre-Kindergarten program was split between two teachers and would end in two weeks. She'd taken the morning session and

Glenda Moore ran the afternoon classes. That had allowed her some time, but not much in the way of research or paperwork would get done with two kids to watch, so the little time she'd set aside just got swallowed up.

How had this happened? She'd dotted her *i*'s and crossed her *t*'s, planning work and application time carefully, knowing her sister was due to deliver a baby, and that the family might need her help at her sister's popular event-planning business. And now...

She couldn't say no to helping with Lily and Javi, even if their story didn't break her heart. The fact that it *did*, and that she actually liked their somewhat blustery Italian great-aunt, added to the weight of responsibility.

And then her uncle had relegated her to working with an uptight, full-of-himself financial whiz, and if he glanced at his pricey watch again, she would be tempted to kick him in the shin, just to wake him up to reality. The fact that he was to-die-for handsome with dark chocolate eyes, café au lait skin and rumpled black hair would make heads turn in their thriving summer town.

But not hers, because people whose main goal was amassing wealth annoyed her. How could he be thriving in New York and ignoring his mother's failing business and health in the Finger Lakes? What kind of person did that?

This couldn't possibly be happening, and yet—it just had. Cruz Maldonado didn't look too happy. Well, neither was she, but she understood that Lily and Javier were in need. Their plight took precedence.

"Miss Rory?"

Lily's plaintive voice melted Rory's heart. She bent

low and snugged an arm around the girl's thin shoulders. "What's up, darling?"

"Javi *might* be scared." Lily kept her voice soft, her gaze down, not looking up at Cruz. "Like, not much, but…" She leaned in close. "Just a little bit. Maybe."

Three-year-old Javier didn't look scared.

If anything he looked energized, while Lily looked nervous. "There is no reason to be scared, my little friends, because we are going to have ourselves…" She paused, building their anticipation. "An adventure!"

"A 'venture?" Javier's smoke-toned eyes opened wide. "For weal? I wuv 'ventures so much!"

"With him?" Lily glanced up at Cruz and scrunched her face, clearly unconvinced.

"So it would seem." Rory took Lily's hand, then stood and took Javier's on the other side. "Lily, Javier." She stood as straight and tall as a five-foot-three-inch person could and faced Rosa's tall, broad-shouldered, successful son. "This is your cousin Cruz."

"Hey, guys." He crouched down to meet the kids at their level. "I was friends with your mommy when we were little."

"You know our mommy?" Excitement heightened Lily's voice, as if finding someone acquainted with her mother wasn't the norm. "You played with her?"

"We climbed trees and played in the big barn, and fed goats and chased kittens and trimmed a lot of grapevines in our time," he told her.

"Our mom was wittle?" Javier eyed him with frank suspicion, as if the words didn't quite compute.

"Everybody is a little kid at one time," Rory reminded them. "We start as babies, then we grow to be kids."

"Then big kids," added Lily.

"And then we get to be moms and dads!" Javier added that last with all the excitement he could muster. "I'm Javier and I'm th-this many." He held up five fingers, then forced his thumb down with his other hand. "Four."

"Almost four. In three months," Rory reminded him.

"Th-that's right. Free months."

Lily pointed up at the clock on the wall. "Can we go back to be with Mimi now?" She looked from Steve to Rory, ignoring Cruz. "I just want to be back with her and I think it's time."

"Me, too." Javier's voice choked slightly. "I miss my Gator so much."

Rory caught Cruz's sympathetic expression, and acted quickly. Something about these kids seemed to touch a nerve in him. A nerve that said the hard-jawed, grim-faced man might actually have a heart.

She bent between the two kids and kept her voice teacher-firm as her brother-in-law entered the room. "You can't go back and live with Rosa right now."

"Is she in trouble?"

Leave it to Lily to get straight to the point, but Rory wasn't about to explain all of the legal issues to the kids, so she opted for plan B. "You know she hasn't been feeling well."

Both kids knew that firsthand. They nodded, solemn.

"While the doctors figure out what to do, she needs some extra rest, so you guys are going to stay at my house. You can help me get things ready for school each day, and help me take care of my dog, okay? As an added bonus, we get to walk all over town together.

And, Javier, we'll have someone bring Gator over to my house." She aimed a reassuring look his way. "And anything else you guys need."

"You live in the village?" Cruz asked.

She raised her eyes to his. "On Creighton Landing, just beyond The Square."

"It's late," he went on. He swept the kids a quick look before he turned his attention back to her. "Can we meet tomorrow and talk this through? I'm a little unprepared and that's not my norm."

She was pretty sure it wasn't his norm, because no one rose to the heights of financial security that quickly without being prepared for everything, all the time. "I'm done with school at noon, so the kids and I should get back to my house by twelve thirty or so."

"And they're okay with you for the day?"

Was he missing the basic meaning of shared custody? She bit back words of protest because anything was doable for a day. "For tomorrow, yes."

"Thank you, Miss Gallagher."

"Rory." She let go of Javier and put out her hand. "As their teacher I'm a mandated reporter. A circumstance which brought us to this moment. I'm afraid your mother is very angry with me right now."

"As her only child, I'm familiar with the feeling," he told her. "And I think it's highly possible that you are as confounded as I find myself by this sudden change in affairs." He took her hand in his.

She wasn't sure what she expected. A cool, hard handshake, quick and businesslike? Or a quick touch of fingers, as if too busy?

She got neither.

He wrapped her hand in his and studied her for long,

slow seconds. Did he like what he saw, or was he as-sessing an adversary? She couldn't tell, and that didn't sit well with the youngest Gallagher sister. She hadn't been gifted with the business acumen her mother and older sister Kimberly possessed, a talent they used to run a mega-successful wedding and event-planning business.

And she didn't have the stage presence and eye for fashion of her middle sister Emily, now a bridal shop owner.

Rory had gotten Gram Gallagher's help-for-the-downtrodden heart, but right now her goal might be ruined by lack of time and available real estate. With her mother away, and Kimberly's baby due soon, she would most likely be adding time spent at Kate & Company to her jam-packed days, further dwindling her grant application period.

She couldn't let that happen. Kids were depending on her, counting on her to provide strong early edu-cation for needy families tucked within the hills sur-rounding Grace Haven. She'd put things off while her dad fought brain cancer in Houston for the past year. Now that he was in remission, her time had come.

Or so she'd thought.

She held Cruz's gaze.

He'd read the reaction she tried to hide. Rory wasn't sure if that was good or bad. She *had* been taken by surprise, but would she have refused to help?

No.

For now she was going to drive home and get these two kids tucked into bed.

Then she'd sit down and start praying, because her life just got put on hold once more. And to tell the truth, Rory Gallagher was tired of having decisions jerked out from under her. "It's not the first U-turn I've made." She addressed Cruz with a cool tone. "And I expect it won't be the last." She slanted a smile to the children and gave a light squeeze to their linked hands. "But it might just be the most fun." She turned to her brother-in-law, the new Grace Haven chief of police. "Drew, feel free to catch me up on things as they develop."

"Drew Slade?" A look of recognition lightened Cruz's face as he turned to Drew. "It's been a long time."

"It has, man." Drew flashed Cruz a quick smile, then waved Rory off. "I'll catch up with you later. Are you all set with them?"

He meant the kids, and despite the fact that Rory's life had just been steamrollered, she was more than willing to take care of these sweet souls. "I am. I'll leave you guys to the legalese." She looked down and smiled at two confused preschoolers. "It's almost time for bed."

"Good night, guys. Sweet dreams." Uncle Steve waved as the other men dove deep into discussion of the whys and hows of the situation.

These kids didn't need to hear conversations about themselves. It wasn't until she'd gotten both kids through the town hall entrance that they were blessed with quiet, the strong male voices muted by distance.

"Come on, guys. Let's call it a day, shall we?"

Javier looked around, confused.

Lily tried to look brave, but her lower lip quivered as the five-year-old fought tears.

Rory led the kids to her car, tucked them into the seats she'd borrowed from the fire hall and drove home because there really wasn't any other choice.

Chapter Two

Cruz took the right-hand turn along the lake's western shore, determined to ferret out the facts of the situation from his mother.

She wouldn't want to see him. She'd made that abundantly clear in the past. They'd fought after his father's death, and Rosa had ordered him out of the house and out of her life, then spent years ignoring his attempts at reconciliation. Funny how a woman who professed faith in the Bible shrugged off forgiveness in favor of old-world pride.

He pulled into the curved drive leading into Casa Blanca and hit the brakes hard in disbelief.

Flaking, peeling paint marred the front of the house. Weeds and grass had infiltrated the once pristine gardens, while twining roses fought a losing battle with invasive weeds, climbing and choking the once beautiful trellises.

Beyond the curving drive and parking lot, both in need of repair and sealing, his father's previously impeccable vineyard stood ragged. Overgrown vines stuck out at odd angles, choking and shading the growing fruit below. The barns didn't look too bad, their paint appeared more recent, but the once prestigious event center had fallen into grave disrepair.

He'd only been gone eight years. How could things have gone this bad in eight short years?

The front door opened.

His mother emerged.

She stared at him as he pulled the car into the drive. Arms folded tight around her middle, she stood straight, solid and self-protective as he exited the car and walked her way. "Hello, Mother. Long time, no see."

She glared at him, then the upscale car, then him again. "You've come to brag, no doubt. To laugh in the face of my ruination. Well, have your say and get out. There's nothing for you here."

Was there ever?

Yes, when his father was alive. His father loved to spend time with his only son, seeing and doing things together, learning "the grape" as he called it. He'd spent long hours working side by side with his father, a master vineyard manager, an immigrant success story. And while they'd worked the grape, his mother had managed the sprawling event center she'd inherited from her parents.

He longed to sass her back in kind. If asked, he would have sworn he'd gotten over all of this years ago, but he was mistaken because the urge to argue with his mother was on the tip of his tongue.

Then he remembered Reverend Gallagher's words that morning. *Your mother is sick. Her heart is bad and she's diabetic, and there are two illegal immi-*

grant children living with her. She needs you, Cruz. And Elina's children need you, too.

He hadn't even known Elina had children. If pressed, he wouldn't have been able to say what his cousin had done once she'd left for Mexico…but what were her children doing here, and what happened to Elina? "How are you?"

The simple question took her by surprise, but not for long. "I am fine. The children and I are fine."

A lie. Again, no surprise. "Reverend Gallagher says you've been ill."

"I have my days. Some good, some bad. Why are you here? Did he call you?"

Cruz nodded.

"He shouldn't have done that. He should have left things be."

"Well, the thought of you serving a jail sentence for harboring illegal immigrants weighed on his conscience. He is, after all, a minister."

She scowled. "He's a neighbor first, a man who knows you have no respect for the mother who gave you life and raised you. Steve knows this, and yet he still makes the call." She raised her chin, a classic move. "I can't imagine what he was thinking."

She needed help in more ways than one. Her Italian skin tones were usually deeply tanned by this time of summer. Today she looked pale, and the threadbare pants and loose shirt she wore had seen a lot of use. Always stocky, she'd put on weight since the funeral. The changes in her appearance reflected the ones on the estate. "I told Steve I would help."

She scowled. Her face darkened. "And as I have said before, I don't need your help, Crusberto."

The cold anger in her face used to break his heart. No more.

He'd moved beyond her reach, and her tirades meant nothing now. "You're wrong. You do need my help. The place is a mess, and my guess is you tried to overmanage everything like you usually do, your workers quit and you got yourself into debt trying to recover. But now you're in too deep and there's no way out, and you've got two kids to watch. How am I doing so far?"

She unwound her arms and fisted her hands. "You checked up on me."

"No." When she almost relaxed, he added, "I had my office assistant check up on you while I drove here, so the fact that you are bordering on bankruptcy and your business is uncared for tells me you're on the brink of disaster. If we throw a double federal offense onto the table for willfully harboring two illegal aliens and passing them off as your grandchildren..." He set one foot on the lowest step of what had been a gracious, columned porch, leaned in and said, "You're wrong, Mother. You do need me, like it or not." He straightened and shoved his hands into his pockets as memories surged. "Honestly, if it was just you, I'd walk away, like you did to me so many times, but it's not just you. There are two little kids involved, who deserve a better chance than they've gotten so far, and who've done nothing to deserve being raised by you."

He expected her to lash out. He was prepared for that. What he wasn't prepared for were the tears.

Her hands lost their tension.

Tears streamed down her cheeks in silent succession.

Rosa Maria Maldonado didn't cry. Ever. To see her come undone messed him up.

He took a step back, then forward, but what could he do? They hadn't comforted one another for a very long time.

He stood absolutely still as her tears flowed. Somewhere deep inside, a tiny longing to help ignited.

He extinguished it quickly. He'd learned how to protect himself decades ago. He'd steeled himself to pretend her indifference didn't matter. He pretended he didn't care.

She swiped the back of her hand to her face, turned around and walked back inside. The door closed behind her, and the click of the lock slipped into place.

So be it. She didn't need him. He didn't need her. But those two children needed something more than to be made wards of the court and deported.

He strode back to his car, got in and drove away to find a hotel room. It took him less than an hour to realize the entire town was booked solid.

Of course everything was taken—it was midsummer at one of the most beautiful lakeside recreation spots in Central New York, the heart of the Finger Lakes.

He sighed and pinched the bridge of his nose. Ten hours ago he'd been gearing up to oversee the takeover of a small dot-com company. That single acquisition was going to make their firm millions.

But he wasn't on Liberty Street, signing the final papers. He'd left that to others. He was here in Grace Haven, a place he'd vowed to never see again.

He got into the car, hit a phone app and came up with no vacancies surrounding the lake. So where could he stay?

Hello, Captain Obvious. Your mother's got room.

Plenty of room. Why don't you pretend to be a peace-maker and go back there?

He'd sleep in the car first. And that's exactly what he intended to do, except then his phone rang with a call from Drew Slade.

"Cruz, it's Drew. I just realized you might not be comfortable staying at Casa Blanca…"

That meant his reaction to his mother showed, and Cruz never let reactions show. It was this stupid town, and these throwback circumstances undermining his skills as a stone-faced negotiator. "My wife and I just vacated a nice little garage apartment at the Gallagh-ers'."

"Is that an inn?"

"No, the Gallagher family. At Chief Gallagher's house. I married his oldest daughter, Kimberly."

"The Gallaghers, as in the holier-than-thou school-teacher I just met?"

"That's Rory." Drew sounded almost cheerful about it. "Anyway, Kimberly and I are in our new house, the apartment is in great shape, and if you really don't want to stay with your mother, this could give you some peace of mind and a clean pillow. I know the town is booked up. Summer is a crazy-busy vacation time here."

It was vacation time in New York City, too, which was the only reason he was able to be here, and not in the city. His boss would no doubt go ballistic when he returned from his three-week European vacation and found Cruz still in Grace Haven. But with Rod-ney Randolph, ballistic was often the status quo. He'd deal with that as needed. "I don't want to be an incon-venience to anyone, Drew."

"The place is empty, you're inconveniencing no one, and if you and Rory are sharing kid duty until we figure things out, you might as well be geographically close."

That part made sense, and was about the only thing in this convoluted mess that did.

"Were you able to find a room for tonight?"

Cruz couldn't lie. "No."

"Then use it, man. One forty-seven Creighton Landing, just beyond the turnoff for The Square, in walking distance of everything. Just like Manhattan." Drew laughed, and Cruz was glad someone found humor in this situation, because he hadn't stopped frowning since the reverend's phone call that morning.

"You sure no one will mind?"

"Positive. I'll call Rory and let her know so you don't surprise her or the kids. Or Mags."

"Is Mags one of the sisters?" Somewhere in his brain he remembered several Gallagher sisters.

"She's a member of the family, all right," Drew finished cryptically. "The key is hanging inside the carriage house, to the left of the door when you walk in. The apartment is the second floor."

Cruz hesitated, then accepted. "Thanks, man. I was ready to sleep in the car."

"Glad to help. I'm hoping this all looks better in the morning."

"It couldn't look any worse."

Wrong again.

He'd driven to Creighton Landing, found the key like Drew said and thrown open a couple of windows in hopes of a lake breeze.

Nope.

Too tired to care, he'd fallen into bed, then got up crazy early like he always did and set up his laptop in the steamy apartment.

No air-conditioning.

No Wi-Fi.

He stared at the screen, searched for networks and didn't find any. He pulled out his smartphone to set up a hot spot to relay internet service.

It didn't work. His phone indicated internet service in the area, but couldn't command a strong enough signal to relay Wi-Fi to the laptop.

He needed to punch someone. And find coffee.

Coffee. A coffee shop with Wi-Fi. Perfect.

He stepped outside with his small laptop bag. The town lay before him, and the lake spread out to his left, just beyond Route 20.

He'd be silly to drive because he was already in town, so he crossed the yard and circled The Square, a local old-time shopping area that looked much more upscale than he remembered, and hunted for coffee.

Nothing was open.

He glared at his phone. It was 6:05 a.m. on a Tuesday. He'd passed two coffee shops, neither of which opened for nearly an hour. In Manhattan, he'd have been connected and working already. Here?

Nothing.

He was about to retrace his steps, get into the car and head toward the thruway, when lights flickered on at the diner just ahead. "You lookin' for coffee?" A copper-skinned, middle-aged woman with dark hair in a bun poked her head around the corner of the stoop.

"Hunting would be more apt," he told her as he strode forward. "And Wi-Fi. Do you have that, too?"

She laughed and swung the door wide. "We're connected, though I'm not sure it was a good idea. Come on in. You looked like a wanderin' pup out there. It's always the same with big-city types. It takes a day or two of bein' in Grace Haven to realize it's okay to relax. To let go and let God shape the days."

"Well, I'm in town for a while, but I'm not sure relaxing enters into the equation."

"Never does at first," she called back as she bustled around the counter. "But we get to it, eventual-like. If we stay 'round long enough." She set a second pot brewing, then toted four mugs and a glass coffee carafe to his table. "Here you go." She filled his cup, then paused. "Room for cream and sugar?"

"Nope. Black."

She sighed as if she expected him to say that, then plunked the other three mugs down on a table kitty-corner from him. She filled the mugs, added a little aluminum pot of cream to the table and strode behind the old-style counter just as three older gentlemen walked in.

"Mornin', Sadie!" crowed the first one in the door.

The next man in seemed just as happy to be there. "Sadie, my sweet Southern belle, you've got us all set up!"

The third man saluted the waitress with his Grace Haven Eagles baseball cap as he came through. "Coffee and Sadie—my mornin's complete!"

"Mornin', boys." She waved a hand as she stuck a paper onto an old-style order ring suspended between her and the kitchen beyond. "I'm orderin' you the usual, speak now or keep it to yourself when you get same old, same old."

"Why mess with success?" the first man wondered aloud. The three men settled at the table to Cruz's right, jawing about baseball.

Cruz opened his computer and brought up his email. One message in, the second guy stood and came up alongside Drew's table. "You got box scores on that thing?"

"Excuse me?" Surprise toughened Cruz's voice. Either surprise, or his Wall Street, tough-as-nails attitude. Bright blue eyes under faded brows gazed back at him from a face that had known years of weathering. "I expect they're accessible."

"Bring 'em up, why don't you, so I can show these yahoos what I mean 'bout the All-Star break makin' a difference."

"He's workin', Badge," Sadie scolded the older man from her spot at the counter. She was slicing big, thick wedges of pie, wrapping them gently and placing them in a tall rotating cooler. Seeing them made Cruz remember the mouth-watering pie at his mother's table, thick and sweet. There was no such thing as good pie in Manhattan. In a city that claimed to boast everything good, pie hadn't made the list. "I don't think he lugged that machine in here to jaw about the American League East with you. Best leave him to it, don't you think?"

"I get your point, Sadie. Smart as always." The old man accepted her advice and moved back across the aisle to his table. "I'll let you get on with your day," he added to Cruz.

"If we had one of them smartphones, we'd know

what's up," said the tallest man. "My Kimmie's got one of them, and it's law-awful how quick she can get on things."

"She's connected, sure as shootin'." The third man stared at his coffee, glum. "No regular daily anymore, no local radio shows that do sports, less'n I wanna sit home with the tube on, watchin'. Then it's midmornin' 'fore we get a clean look at who's done what unless you've got cable, and my monthly check don't allow for that kind of indulgence." The old fellow sighed softly, but just loud enough for Cruz to hear.

They were killing him.

Worse?

He knew what they were saying. Times had changed and unless you were familiar with smart technology, you were stuck waiting for access to information in fewer spots than there used to be. He slugged his coffee, pulled up the baseball box scores online and motioned the guys over. "Check it out, boys."

"For real?" They moved, en masse, coffees in hand, and slid into the other three seats at his table.

Sadie came by with more coffee. She caught his gaze and smiled. "Nice."

He hadn't really had a choice, not when they'd started talking baseball. He lived in a city with two of the greatest baseball teams in history, and he hadn't gone to a game. Ever. Time was money in New York.

Time is money anywhere, his conscience reminded him. *But it's more money in Manhattan. You might want to think about why that's become so important.*

He set the open laptop at the end of the table so all three men could see it, and as they jabbered about who'd done what on the West Coast, the diner door opened.

"Well, it looks like the early bird has gone and caught herself two of the sweetest little worms I ever did see!" Sadie exclaimed as Rory Gallagher came in with Lily and Javier. "This is a nice surprise, Rory!"

"My toaster's not working, I had no cereal and I need to feed these two before the school day starts." She smiled down at the kids, back up at Sadie, then she saw him.

Her smile faded, but it brightened again when she spotted the crew at his table. "Good morning, gentlemen."

"If it ain't the prettiest of the Gallagher girls stoppin' by!"

"Ain't them Rosa's younguns?"

"They are." Rory said nothing about yesterday's drama. "They get to stay with their teacher for a little bit. How cool is that?"

"I think it's a fine thing, Miss Rory." The blue-eyed man seemed to understand more of what had transpired than the others. "A perfect place to grow and run and laugh while the dust settles."

"Thank you, Badge."

He didn't nod or smile, but the old guy's expression indicated approval. He slugged more coffee, then stood. "Boys, let's get up and make some room here. Miss Rory needs a place to sit with the kids."

"With all them empty seats?" Surprised, the taller man swept the mostly empty restaurant a quick glance.

Rory waved them off and indicated the next booth. "We can sit here. That way the kids can see Cruz while he works." She flashed him a cool look of dismissal, as if working on a weekday morning was the root of all evil. Last time Cruz looked, it was considered normal, but he closed the laptop and faced her as the men moved back to their original table.

She didn't sit with him. She herded the kids into the adjacent booth, ordered eggs and pancakes and orange juice for Lily and Javier, and coffee for herself.

Was she not hungry? Or broke?

Only one way to find out. He stood and slipped into her booth, next to Lily. "Morning, guys."

Javier stared at him, uncertain. Lily looked less concerned. "Miss Rory told us that you know our Mimi."

"Mimi?"

"Rosa," Rory explained softly. "That's what they call her."

"Not Abuela?"

Rory met his gaze, and realization sank in. "Of course, Elina's mother would have been Abuela."

"And they started with Mami for Rosa, but Javier morphed it to Mimi and it stuck."

"Your Mimi is my mother." Cruz looked down at Lily. Elina's eyes gazed up at him. His heart winced a little more as he thought of his cousin's choices. "And your mommy was my friend and my cousin."

"She died." Javier announced the words in a voice that showed a lack of understanding. "She might come back. She might not. Mimi doesn't know."

Lily leaned across the table, so serious. "No one can come back when they die, Javi. They have to go live with God in heaven and there's no way back."

The little guy's face darkened. He stared at his sister and whispered, "She might come back, Lily. She might."

Cruz's chest went tight. Seeing Elina's fate through the eyes of two innocent children, emotion gripped him.

They loved his mother.

The irony of that didn't sit well, because he could look back and count the few happy times on his fingers. His mother had been a tough taskmaster, a woman overseeing a burgeoning business overlooking Canandaigua Lake, and nothing mattered more than her success. Her vineyard, her special events center, was straight out of the hills of Tuscany. Casa Blanca meant more to her than anything. More than her hardworking Latino husband, and certainly more than her only son.

But these children seemed bonded to her. Was it an act? Or had Rosa Maldonado changed?

He had no way of knowing, but he wasn't about to let two innocents go through similar experiences. Not if she was still the tough, overbearing, money-solves-everything woman he remembered.

Rory slipped an arm around Javier and drew him close. "No matter what happens here on earth, God's in heaven watching over us. Smiling down at us, wanting us to be happy and strong. And now your mama is there with him, loving you from up there. But here on earth, God has other folks to love you. Lily, Mimi, Cruz and me, just to name a few. You will always be our beloved little boy. That will never change, darling."

The little guy nestled into the curve of her arm. "I know." The two words came out in a whisper. "I just miss her, is all."

Cruz's eyes got misty.

Sadie saved the moment by slipping two plates of

pancakes and scrambled eggs in front of the kids, then refilling the grown-ups' mugs. "Rory, you sure I can't get you somethin', darlin'?"

Rory shook her head. "I'm fine, Sadie, thanks."

"All right, sweetie."

Sweetie. Darlin'. Sweet things... Cruz couldn't remember the last time someone called him sweetie in New York. Probably never. Because why would they?

And yet it seemed real nice to hear those words here.

Lily knelt up on the booth's seat to get a better vantage point on her food. Her first attempt at the eggs had them sliding to the floor quickly. Cruz handed her his spoon. "Try this. Eggs are slippery."

"They are!" She accepted the spoon and didn't seem to mind that he'd stirred his coffee with it. "And they jiggle. Jell-O jiggles, too. I like jiggly food."

Rory laughed.

Cruz lifted his eyes to hers. "Jiggly food is funny?"

"My sister won't eat food that jiggles. She says it's unnerving. I'm happy to see Lily has no such qualms."

"Did they sleep well?"

"As well as any of us could with a crazy day behind us and a new normal awaiting. I expect tonight will be better. Drew called and told me he offered you the carriage house apartment."

"I'll find a hotel as soon as I can, so I'm not inconveniencing anyone." Cruz sipped his coffee. "No reason to make difficult circumstances more so."

"Why stay somewhere else when you can stay there for free?" She looked puzzled, as if the idea of spending money worried her. So maybe she did like breakfast and couldn't afford it, but sacrificed for the two kids.

Now he felt like a complete moron.

"I need internet access and there's no air-conditioning."

She sat back and looked distressed. "The window unit."

"Excuse me?"

"Drew took it out last fall and stored it downstairs over the winter, and then they moved into their new house before it got hot. I forgot all about that, and I'm sure he did, too. Oh, Cruz." She leaned forward, and looked honestly concerned. "You must have roasted."

"I may have discovered a new scientific melting point."

She laughed again, and when she did, the kids smiled. Her laugh made him feel like smiling, too, and that felt good and odd because the rigors of Manhattan didn't often inspire laid-back conversation and smiles. "Listen, it would be silly of you to waste money on a hotel when I expect you'd like to get to know these guys better, right?"

He knew less than nothing about children which meant he'd be of little help. "I guess."

"I'll have our house Wi-Fi upgraded so you can access it in the apartment. They should probably be able to do that today. The air-conditioning unit cools off the whole place. Can you install it in the living room window or do you need help?"

How hard could it be? "I expect I can manage it."

"If it's too tricky or awkward, wait till I get home with these guys later. I'll be glad to jump in."

"Miss Wory, can I have more syrup?" Javier asked.

Cruz waited for her to say no. Every young mother he knew measured out anything sweet in minute doses, as if sugar had become the root of all evil.

"Of course you can!" Rory helped Javier with the

little glass carafe, then reached for a second one. "Try this triple-berry syrup, too, Javi, on just a little corner here. Or you can dip a piece."

"I wuv dipping!"

"Me, too." She picked up a tiny piece of his pancake, dipped it in the dark purple syrup and popped it into her mouth. "Perfection." She smiled at Lily, then Javier.

"Are you walking straight to school from here?" Cruz asked.

She nodded. "The White Church, actually, on Maple Avenue. They volunteered to house us in their basement this year."

"Basement?" School in a basement didn't sound like much fun.

She scrunched up her nose when she frowned. "We're an itinerant program, which means we get shuffled from place to place every summer. Whatever church or school has extra space is where we're assigned, so we've learned to bloom where we're planted."

"That's a little rough."

She shrugged. "It's not ideal, but we manage to make do. When I'm planning, I make sure we've got so much to do, say and learn that the location becomes a nonproblem. I wasn't able to get any prep work done yesterday, so we're walking over early today. That way I can get things ready."

"You do the morning sessions?"

She nodded. "Another teacher steps in to take the afternoon ones. That way we can cover for one another as needed."

"What will the kids do in the afternoon?"

"Hang with me, I expect. Unless you have a better idea?"

He knew what he should say. He should offer to take the kids off her hands for the afternoon.

His phone signaled an incoming text, then another, and that made his decision easy. He had work. So did she. But hers was geared toward little kids. His wasn't. He stood, determined to claim what time he could. "You can never get enough learning, can you?"

His answer disappointed her, but she didn't seem surprised, which meant she expected him to be self-centered. Like mother, like son?

He bit back remorse because he recognized the pattern quite well, thank you.

"Enjoy your day," she told him. "We'll see you this afternoon. And if you need help with that AC unit, I'll be home midday. Also, if you need Wi-Fi, you can hole up in one of the empty corners of Kate & Company, my mother's event-planning business on The Square."

He remembered the name well. Her mother's business had used his parents' classic villa and vineyard for many events when he was younger. "Your mom wouldn't mind?"

"She's retired, my sisters are handling the business and there's an extra office on the first level. It's small, but it's cool and connected."

Cool and connected.

The phrase sounded almost insulting, as if a good working environment was a bad thing.

He slipped his laptop into its leather case. His objective in Grace Haven was to get his mother out of legal jeopardy and arrange care for Elina's children. It was the least he could do to repay Elina's friendship.

After that he'd return back to life as he knew it. The life he'd been thrust into years ago, because being good was never good enough for Rosa Maldonado. Not when being the best dangled like the perfect cluster of Champagne grapes, just out of reach. He paid for his coffee, and her bill, too, then offered the kids a quick wave as he strode out the door.

He wasn't sure why he was leaving, when he'd intended to hang out in there, drinking what had turned out to be really solid coffee and using their Wi-Fi. He walked back down the street, turned toward Creighton Landing and decided to install the AC unit sooner rather than later. Then he'd approach Drew's wife at Kate & Company about leasing office space while he was here. Rory Gallagher hadn't mentioned a price tag on her offer, but Cruz understood that nothing was free in the corporate world, and if he paid his way, there were fewer emotional entanglements to worry about. Keeping life unemotional had worked well so far. Cruz Maldonado had every intention of keeping things that way.

Chapter Three

Edgy, well-to-do and intent on working from dawn till dark.

Guys like Cruz Maldonado didn't pause to smell the roses because they never looked down long enough to notice them. The guy wore his money-first mentality like Gucci armor, unsoftened by his heart-stopping good looks. His black hair was shaggy in the back, as if he was too busy to notice.

But Rory noticed right off, unfortunately, because the look worked for him and she had to remind herself that he was off-limits.

His complexion was the kind that tanned easily, although his hadn't darkened appreciably and it was already midsummer. That meant he spent way too much time indoors.

Those gorgeous brown eyes, soulful but sharp, were brightened by hints of gold around the pupil. Thick, dark brows defined those eyes with a decisive arch. He was eye candy, all right, which Rory found annoying. And now he was going to be underfoot, tucked in their carriage house apartment because her brother-in-law Drew thought it was a good idea.

It was a horrible idea.

But smart, too, because with Kimberly's baby due, Rory might have to help her sister Emily run the event-planning business their mother had built. Kimberly had taken on Kate & Co. a year ago as their father fought brain cancer in a Texas treatment center, but she'd need time off now and the girls had pledged support for one another while their father recovered.

"Miss Rory, you're not hungry?" Lily settled her hand on Rory's forearm. "Not even a little bit?"

"I'm not a breakfast eater, darling."

"Mimi says we have to eat in the morning." Javier stared at his almost full plate and frowned. "I weally like just playing in th-th-the morning." A tiny stutter plagued him when he got nervous or tired. "I wike that the most."

Rory sympathized completely. "We'll have Sadie box that up and you can have it at snack time, okay?"

"Weally?" His face perked up. "You don't mind?"

"Dude, I get really annoyed when people push food on me. I know when I'm hungry. I know when I'm not. We're all different, right?"

"Sure!" He looked downright excited by the thought of having a choice in the matter.

Sadie came by just then. "I heard those words of wisdom and I'll take care of that right now, darlins. Lily, I cannot believe you wolfed that down. You go, girl!"

"I love pancakes!" Lily almost sang the words. "And I love coming to fancy restaurants and having food, Sadie! Thank you for being so nice to us!"

"Oh, my sweet thing." Sadie crossed back to the counter, flipped out a foam to-go box and came back to the table as more folks filtered in through the door. "It is my sincere pleasure to be nice to my customers."

"It is?" Javier peeked up as if her words were really special.

"Indeed. I am not one to blow sunshine at anyone, my friend. If Sadie says it—" the robust woman put her hands on her hips and offered Javier a sage expression "—Sadie means it."

"It's my p-p-pleasure to come here, too." Javier dimpled when he told her, clearly pleased. "It's s-s-such a nice place, Sadie."

"Oh, you precious little thing!" Sadie beamed at them, then started walking away.

Rory called her back. "Sadie, I need the check. Is it in your pocket?"

"No check today, honey. A kindly benefactor has taken care of it."

Did she just say the check had been paid? The only person who'd gone near the cash register was Cruz. She didn't need him to buy her breakfast; she wasn't broke, she was financially challenged. She'd avoided a full-time teaching position because she had other plans, plans that were being threatened, yet again.

Sue Collingsworth stepped into the diner as they were sliding out of the booth. She looked totally put together, like always. A stab of guilt dredged up a wave of emotion inside Rory, exacerbated by current events with Lily and Javier.

She'd longed for Sue's friendship in junior high. She'd have done anything to hang out with the cool crowd, the gorgeous girls who were always in the know about everything. She'd thought so much about looks and reputation back then that she'd sacrificed her one true friend: Millicent Rodriguez, the daughter of a Dominican maid at the elegant Lakeside Inn. They'd been inseparable as kids, romping down the beach, dashing back and forth between the stately inn and Rory's house.

And then she'd messed it all up by wanting to be part of the cool crowd.

So young. So foolish. And utterly selfish.

She'd been accepted by the cool crowd, probably because her sister had been a pageant queen. But they'd shunned Millicent.

And so had she.

When her childhood friend ended up dead from a drug overdose fifteen months later, Rory had to face the consequences of her actions. Would Millicent have joined the drug crowd if Rory had stuck by her?

Probably not, and the truth of that had stayed with Rory all this time. Now it was her turn to make a difference, and her planned preschool and kindergarten would do just that.

"Rory." Susan lifted two perfect brows slightly, almost as if pained to acknowledge her presence. "How are you?"

"Fine, thank you. And—"

"Miss Wory! I've got to go potty, bad!"

Susan noted the presence of the children as if suffering stomach pangs, and when Lily reached out a hand to touch the sparkles running from shoulder to hip on her dress, Susan stepped back to avoid contact.

She was a rude, insufferable person back then, and

not much had changed, but Rory had followed her around like a needy pup. No more.

She stooped low to reassure the little fellow. "Well, let's take care of that before we walk to school, okay, my friend?"

Javi did a dance-hop step of urgency, nodding.

"May I sit at the counter while you go?" Lily climbed onto one of the taller counter stools. "I can talk to Miss Sadie, and twirl!" She spun the seat around, laughing.

"Yes, but keep your feet tucked so people can get around you. And use your indoor voice, remember?"

Lily nodded, and put two hands over her mouth. "Got it," she whispered, grinning.

Susan said nothing more.

Just as well. They really had nothing to say to one another beyond hello. She walked Javi to the restrooms, then afterward held his hand while they strolled toward the White Church.

She'd learned a harsh lesson at a young age.

She'd watched the well-to-do crowd hurt other kids' feelings, and had done nothing to stop it. She'd watched them reject kids who didn't have as much, then treat them as failures. And when Millicent succumbed to an overdose, Rory had understood the tragic results of inaction. When Lily revealed that her mother had gone to heaven, Rory had had a major wake-up call.

Rosa didn't have legal guardianship, and the children's paperwork had been misrepresented. As a teacher, she was required to be upfront and honest, which meant if these kids needed help, she'd be wrong to deny it to them.

If Rosa had obeyed the law, there would have been no mess to unravel, but she hadn't and Rory had had no choice but to reveal the information to authorities two days ago.

"Miss Rory?"

"Yes, Lily?" She tipped her gaze down. Two sad brown eyes gazed up at her.

"Thank you for letting us stay with you." She gripped Rory's hand tighter in a show of emotion. "I would have been a little scared with someone else. Except Mimi," she amended quietly. "But I don't like being with strangers."

"I don't wike them, either." Javier shook his head with boyish vehemence. "I just wike people I know."

"And let us not grow weary of doing good..." Paul's words, as he reminded the Galatians to keep heart. As Lily clung to one hand and Javier gripped the other, emotion welled within her. She would put their needs first, and somehow, someway, she'd finagle time to get the paperwork done and submitted to the state before the deadline. If it meant little sleep for a few weeks, well...

That was the sacrifice she'd have to make. As they walked south on Main Street, Flora Belker flagged her down. "Rory, got a minute?"

She didn't, but she'd make time for Flora. Flora and Rory's grandmother had been best friends since childhood, and when Grandma Gallagher came up to visit from her retirement spot on Florida's Gulf Coast, she and Flora would sit, laugh and talk for hours. Flora missed Maddie Gallagher tremendously. "Of course I do! What's up?"

"I am fit to be tied." Flora had been watering her lawn, always lush and green and weed-free, but she turned the water off and braced her hands on her hips.

"My brother is finally getting his way and the Belker block is going to go up for sale despite my objections."

"He got your sister to agree?" The three Belkers had inherited the multibuilding estate years ago, but had never been able to agree on much of anything. While Leroy had wanted to sell, the ladies hadn't, and Thelma had been staunchly opposed to any kind of change for years. "How'd he do that?"

"After all this time she's gotten a bee in her bonnet about moving to a Florida retirement community not far from your grandparents. A significant cash settlement would help buy her way in, and while I say good for her, the thought of that property going to a stranger is just breaking my heart."

She looked more angry than heartbroken, and Rory knew what it was like to be odd man out with siblings now and again. She made a face of regret, but said, "You knew you wouldn't be able to hang on to it forever, Flora. And you've got this place." Rory swept Flora's stately nineteenth-century home an admiring look. "And you told me yourself that keeping up both places had gotten to be too much for you."

"But that didn't mean I wanted my family heritage sold out from under me," the older woman retorted.

"Of course not." Rory nodded, sympathetic, but then an idea occurred to her. An amazingly wonderful, brilliant idea. "Miss Flora, are you guys selling the property as one unit or would you consider subdividing?"

"Obviously I'm not in the know about anything because I didn't agree with the notion of selling in the first place, but I don't think they care how it gets sold as long as it does," she declared. "I'm just beside my-

self, but that's not a worry to either one of them, more's
the pity!"

Maddie Gallagher had been the softhearted one of
the trio, Flora Belker the tough girl who stayed single
all these years and Thelma Brown the happy-go-lucky
one. They'd hung together for years, but with Maddie
and Thelma both in Florida, Flora would be left behind, and that might be part of the angst. Still, if they
would be willing to subdivide the commercially zoned
property, the original Belker home was a quaint one-
story set on a grassy slope, easily accessible from the
road behind Main Street, ideal for a preschool.

She'd call Melanie Carson, a popular local Realtor
and her mother's good friend. If Melanie could put in
an offer for part of the parcel, Miss Flora might not
feel so bad about the changes. A former schoolteacher
herself, she might actually like the idea of their old
home becoming a preschool.

Either way, it was worth a shot, because finding
commercially zoned available property in Grace Haven
was next to impossible.

Cruz showed up at the White Church just before
noon. He'd left his car parked in the Gallagher driveway, and walked the four blocks at a brisk pace. When
he arrived at the intersection of Fourth and Maple, he
was almost sorry the walk was done.

Canandaigua Lake lay beyond the church, form-
ing a long, slim, water-filled valley between rolling,
verdant hills, a picture-perfect pocket of Americana.

He walked a lot in Manhattan. Everyone did.

This was different. It smelled, looked and felt different, and the ever-present city sounds he blocked out

so easily had been replaced by birds chirping, kids playing and young mothers chatting as they pushed strollers.

He'd taken a left at Broadway and ended up in the greeting-card setting he'd brushed off for years. Only it was way nicer than he'd remembered, but maybe his memories were tainted by family dynamics. He spotted a hand-printed pre-K sign with an arrow underneath, and followed it to the back entrance of the church. He went through the back door, and down the steps to the church basement.

He didn't need an arrow to find Rory. Her voice filled the space, laughing and singing with the two kids. He almost wanted to hurry, but that would be silly. He wasn't here to mess with her time frame, but to apologize for wrecking her AC unit.

"Cousin Cruz!" Lily spotted him from across the room.

Javier turned, grinned and waved. "You can have wunch wif us! We're having peanut butter and jewwy, and Rory made the jewwy all by herself!"

"It's really good," Lily assured him.

Rory frowned at the clock, then him. "What did you do?"

"What makes you think I did something?"

"You have a guilty look about you."

He sighed and pinched the bridge of his nose. He'd driven corporate moguls crazy with his unreadable face, but here in Grace Haven, it seemed he was an open book. "I may or may not have killed your air-conditioning unit."

"Oops." She grimaced and moved forward. "Are you all right?"

Her question caught him off guard. She didn't ream him out or make fun of him. She went straight to making sure he was okay. "I'm fine. I just lost my grip on it while I was maneuvering it into place, and it fell."

"Oh, dear. Not onto a person, did it? Because that would be bad."

"A fairly old garbage can on the back side of the garage has just become scrap metal."

She waved that off. "As long as it wasn't anything living, it's no biggie. But we need to get you a unit for that apartment. I know how hot it gets up there."

"I bought one."

"Really? So quick?" She handed Javier his sandwich, then a second one to Lily.

"At the strip mall near the thruway. That's all new since I moved away. And the road is four lanes now, not two. And there's a ton of new development outside the village."

"And still a crazy amount of traffic to navigate through in the summer," she noted.

"Is that why the town is thriving?" he asked.

She made a face, considering. "Tourism is at an all-time high. Vacationers, destination weddings, conventions, golf tournaments, holiday functions. With all the event centers overlooking the lakes, it's pretty busy nine months of the year now. Our sleepy little town has come into its own."

It was quite a change from what he remembered, but not in a bad way. He wasn't one of those people who saw progress in a negative light, but he also knew not everyone shared his viewpoint. "Your sister's place seemed busy, too. And she also seemed very pregnant."

Rory laughed. "She is that."

He held his phone up. "I kept this nearby. Just in case."

"We're all a little nervous and wonderfully excited," she admitted. "There hasn't been a baby in the family for ten years, since my niece Tee Tee was born. But I don't expect you walked over here to chat about babies."

"No." He certainly hadn't, but he was pretty sure he had raised the subject. "I just wanted you to know about the AC unit before you came walking up the driveway and saw the carnage by the street, waiting for pickup."

"It will most likely be gone before we get back there," she assured him.

He frowned.

"Scrap pickers. Dumpster divers. Nothing much gets left for garbage pickup. Someone will grab it to reuse."

He couldn't imagine such a thing. "People go around, intentionally picking up garbage?"

"Recyclables. Things with some use. Like in times of war, when everyone saved everything."

He had no idea what she was talking about.

"Use it up, wear it out," she told him. Then she folded her arms across her middle, over the tank top that showed off her small waist. "You don't recycle in Manhattan?"

"Some, sure, but if it's garbage, it's garbage. They pick it up and carry it away."

She sighed, but not one of those weary, long-suffering sighs. This was one of those "you're exasperating and know nothing, so why don't you get on your way" sighs. "Things are different here. I expect it will all come back to you once you've been here awhile."

He didn't plan on staying long, but she could be right. Maybe small-town interaction wouldn't seem so alien in a few days. "I wasn't in town much growing up. I went to school, played baseball with Drew and Dave in the summer when we were young, and basketball in the winter through high school, but once I got older, I worked the grape."

"You worked in the vineyard?"

She looked surprised, as if he was some silver spoon that coasted through life. "Everyone did. The vines were our legacy, the basis for making Casa Blanca great, so yes. I worked. We all worked. And my mother polished her little dynasty like a newly minted coin. As long as everything appeared perfect on the outside, we were doing an okay job."

Sympathy deepened her gaze, but he wasn't after sympathy. He'd learned a lot from his mother. How to work long and hard, and take no prisoners.

She'd been ruthless.

So was he.

But he was also fair. Rosa had spent a lot of her life not playing fair with others. She'd alienated workers, suppliers and other event centers with her strong-armed dealings.

"Mimi says I can work the grape when I get bigger," Lily told him while chewing a bite of sandwich, and he had to admit, the scent of peanut butter with fresh jam enticed him. "If we still have grapes, that is."

Untended vines stopped producing, which meant Rosa was preparing the children for the vineyard's demise. "We'll have to see what happens, okay?"

She met his gaze and nodded, but not because she

agreed. Because what choice did she have, a small child, with others planning her destiny?

His throat went thick.

Allergies? Maybe. But he knew better.

It wasn't allergies causing his discomfort.

It was the reality he saw in Lily's eyes, the uncertainty gazing back at him.

Their destiny lay in his hands.

He'd negotiated multimillion-dollar acquisitions without arching an eyebrow, overseen hedge fund bundles controlling mega-units of the economy without a twitch, but the thought of determining the outcome of two children struck fear into his heart, because Lily and Javi weren't faceless documents, ready for signing.

They were *famiglia*, as his mother would say. And their fate lay squarely on his shoulders.

As he began to cross over to The Square, activity caught his eye across the street. A well-dressed man was setting a for-sale sign into place in front of the old Belker complex, a stretch of retro buildings reaching from one corner to the next. The well-built but worn complex fronted three roads. The buildings weren't historic, or anything unique, but he understood the rarity of a busy block going up for sale in a sought-after area.

He stared, remembering how tough it had been to get a room. Not tough, actually. *Impossible.*

He noted the number in his phone and texted it to Chen, his right-hand man in Lower Manhattan.

Chen, put in an offer for this as a development location, from personal accounts.

He snapped half a dozen pictures from where he was so the Realtor wouldn't know he was interested.

If a seller realized a person of means was showing interest, the price would rise, and Cruz was in the business of making money, not wasting it.

Purchase ASAP for lowest possible price using a proxy, then resell to highest development bidder. Washburn Hotels, Marriott, etc.

If he could avoid the whole town knowing he was behind the quick sale, people wouldn't be up in arms that he was changing a potential eyesore into a beautiful inn or hotel, close to shopping, the lake, amenities and food. Of course there would be a percentage going back into his bank account, but he didn't have to make a fortune on this transaction. He'd deal quick and clean to get things moving along. Why wait?

Chen must have been on his lunch hour because he texted back a reply almost immediately.

On it.

No one was allowed to use personal devices or access websites from the operating floors, so personal calls and texts could only be made and received away from sensitive information.

He crossed the town park within The Square and went back to working from the small office in Kate & Company. His phone rang, midafternoon. He saw Drew Slade's name on the display and took the call. "Drew, I owe you big-time. Your wife's given me office space with internet and AC and I'm within steps of the apartment. She refused my offer to pay, and looks like she's going to deliver that baby momentarily. That's the only part of this whole deal I find disconcerting, by the way."

Drew laughed. "I'm on pins and needles, too, but I pretend not to be. We're grilling tonight at the Gallagher homestead. Show up in the yard and meet the rest of the family. It's a potluck, but my wife is pretending to be health conscious while sneaking brownies on the sly, so our contribution will no doubt be something fresh and green. Don't feel obliged to eat it."

He and his buddies used to gather on rooftop patios and do that kind of thing. When had that stopped? When had he gotten so busy making money that he'd stopped being a friend? "I'm in. What can I bring?"

"Nothing required, but if you feel weird not bringing something, ride over to the Wegmans and grab a deli salad."

He winced, unseen. "All right, I'll whip something up, but I'll need a bigger bowl than what I have in the apartment."

"Grab what you need out of the Gallagher kitchen. If Kate was here, she'd hand you anything you need."

"See you later." He put in two more hours of work, made a much-needed shopping trip to the giant supermarket on Route 20 and got back with just enough time to make his offering.

Once it was done, he strode through the carriage house, and paused.

Wearing a short-sleeve shirt and shorts, Rory was manning the grill, accompanied by a taller woman, her sister Emily.

He'd seen the pictures in the event center, the three Gallagher women, each unique, all gorgeous.

But then Rory raised her head, and suddenly all he could see was her. Watching her, seeing the jut of her chin, the quick smile and the way those honey-toned eyes crinkled at the corners... No, her sisters were fine women, but neither one held a candle to the youngest Gallagher. He was kind of surprised the other men didn't see it.

He wanted to gulp like an adolescent. Reach up and slick back his hair to make sure it looked right.

Ridiculous.

But when he locked eyes with her over the grilling meat and garlic-laced asparagus, it didn't feel silly. It felt significant. And nice. He shifted his focus to meet her sister, but his attention quickly strayed back to amber-brown eyes that seemed to shine a little brighter whenever he was near.

Chapter Four

Rory checked the temperature of the outdoor gas grill before she laid three pounds of Zweigle's hots across the grate. The ideal conditions of sun plus a lake breeze while grilling equaled summer perfection and she'd challenge anyone to argue otherwise.

"Hot dogs?" Her sister Emily cut across the grass from the shopping niche that drew people into town. "Red, white or both?"

Rory smiled. "Both. And Italian sausage."

"Can I call Grant, have him bring the kids?"

"Grant already knows. He's just pulled up," she added as Grant McCarthy's SUV appeared at the corner. "Your cell phone must have locked up again, because everyone else is on board but you. Corinne's bringing dessert along with Callan and Tee, and Kimberly's bringing a veggie tray."

"Veggie trays are not barbecue food." Emily didn't bother pretending indifference. "We need fries or Grandma's hot potato salad, or a nice big antipasto and pasta salad."

"Will this do?"

They both turned as Cruz approached from the garage bearing a large bowl—her mother's bowl, Rory realized as he drew closer—of an amazingly delicious-looking salad. "Where on earth did you find that? Wegmans deli counter?"

"Drew invited me to come meet the family, so I threw this together after work."

He threw it together? As in a man who looked this good and cooked? There had to be some sort of mistake.

Rory didn't have to gauge Emily's reaction, because her sister pinched her.

"Stop." Rory scolded with both a look and her tone, but Emily had never been squelched easily, and it didn't look like that was about to change as she faced the upscale newcomer.

"You're Rosa's son."

"Cruz. And you're Emily. Your pageant pictures are on both levels of Kate & Company."

"Trapped in time!" Emily laughed and extended her hand with all the elegance of the pageant queen she'd been. "Nice to meet you, Cruz. Where are the kids?" She turned back toward Rory as she asked the question, and gave her a sisterly eye roll of approval.

"Drew took them for a walk with Mags while we wait for Kimberly to appear with the veggies. Although I'll scrap the veggies for whatever Cruz has in Mom's bowl."

"Chicken and artichoke salad with kalamata olives, freshly chopped celery, crumbled feta, grape tomatoes and a balsamic dressing."

"You're like a walking, talking cable food show."

"When I wasn't working the grape—" he crossed

to the nearby picnic table and set down the bowl "—I was working in the kitchen. Dish-washing mostly, but now and again the chefs would let me help. I learned a little here, a little there, and when you live in Manhattan, if you can't cook, you're at the mercy of restaurants. It gets old."

"Eating out gets old?" Rory shot him a look of surprise. "Oh, to travel in your world for just a day or two. I expect it wouldn't get old that quickly, would it?"

He laughed, and it wasn't the suave, deep sound she expected, all movie-star friendly. It was boy-next-door normal, as if he *was* normal.

He wasn't.

She'd heard about Rosa's son at length—the older woman's mix of pride and regret. He'd set the financial world on fire in Manhattan. He'd zigzagged his way through a decade-long bull market and made the investment firm and himself significantly richer. He'd stayed away because Rosa had pushed him away, and the older woman's remorse was plain to see.

But this guy had inherited more than his mother's Mediterranean features. He'd inherited her dogged work ethic, the urge to be the best. Rory had shrugged off movers and shakers a long time ago. She was a simple person and the last thing she needed was to go all schoolgirl crush on her co-guardian.

He sniffed the air, crossed to the grill and reached to open it. "May I?"

"Don't tell me you do hot dogs, too?"

He winked.

Her heart stopped midbeat, then started tapping a tarantella in her chest.

Time for a cooldown, because as light and fun as

she tried to be around Lily and Javier, the task they'd been given wasn't to be handled casually. Two children's lives were at stake; their futures might lie in his hands.

No, she'd keep a cool distance between herself and "Romeo" Maldonado.

He was a playmaker, accustomed to getting his way. When it came to those children, she'd do whatever it took to make sure their best interests were served.

Emily followed her inside. "That's Rosa's son? Seriously?"

"Shh. He'll hear you. And what are you doing, fussing over him? You've seen cute guys before." Rory pretended to be bored.

Emily wasn't buying it. "There's cute and then there's should-be-on-the-big-screen handsome, so don't pretend you're immune. I saw the way you looked at him when you thought he wasn't looking."

"He wasn't looking, was he?" Too late, Rory realized she'd been trapped. "Lay off. We've got to work together, and then he goes back to New York, and if I'm really blessed and give up sleep for the next month, I might get the school grant finished. And life as we know it moves on."

"What if the legalities around the kids can't be resolved?" Emily redirected her attention outside, where Javier and Lily skipped up the driveway, looking delightfully normal. Drew and his nearly teenage daughter, Amy, followed, laughing.

But their legal status was in question, and the thought of what might happen to them went beyond worrisome. Did Cruz know his mother had threatened to grab the children and leave town? Uncle Steve had talked her out of it, but Rory had seen the look on Rosa's face. If things looked bad, she might do just that, although where a sixty-four-year-old woman with health problems thought she'd hide with two cute Hispanic kids was anyone's guess.

She'd seen Rosa disappointed, worried, anguished and sorrowful these past few years, but she'd never seen her angry until this week, and when she did, Rory understood the full range of possibilities. If Elina's children were threatened with deportation, Rosa Maldonado might take them and run, and that was something she needed to talk about with Cruz.

"Cruz, would you like to help me put the kids to bed?" Rory posed the question as the summer shadows began to stretch east from the westward-angled sun.

Her request surprised him. He hesitated, then found out Rory Gallagher didn't do well with hesitation.

"That's okay." Dismissive, she tossed a handful of paper plates into the garbage can outside the garage without looking his way. "I'll do it."

"I'll help."

Now *she* hesitated, as if wanting to reject him. Instead she pulled in a deep breath and called for the kids. "Lily. Javi! Say good-night to everyone, please. Time for bed."

Lily came willingly. She looked tired. Was she worn-out by the long day? Guilt swept him for not taking the kids for the afternoon. Maybe he should have gotten them and brought them back here for rest time if Rory had work to do. Kids still took naps, didn't they? But until what age?

He had no idea, and that was only the beginning of what he didn't know about children.

Javi was ignoring Rory, so Cruz crossed the yard, picked him up and held him almost upside down.

"Eee!" The boy screeched with glee, then reached up for Cruz. When he swung the boy upright, Javier wrapped his arms around Cruz's neck and sighed.

A tiny little fellow, cuddling and sighing against his neck.

It felt good.

He hadn't expected that.

It felt right.

That was a bigger surprise.

And when he turned and spotted Lily tucked along Rory's side, something went warm and soft inside him, and Cruz didn't do warm, soft emotions. Ever.

But the sight of Elina's daughter snuggled against Rory seemed more right than he would have imagined.

His phone buzzed. He pulled it out, glanced at the display and grimaced when he saw his boss Rodney's name. The man was micromanaging while on an extended vacation with his wife and kids. "I've got to take this." He set Javier down, and didn't dare make eye contact with the boy, because he'd feel guilty if he did and phone calls with Rodney rarely went well. Rodney wasn't the kind of man who took family seriously, unless it was his own, and personal time was a nonexistent concept at Randolph & Gordon.

"Come on, honey." Rory took Javier's hand in one of hers, and Lily's in the other. "Javi, you get to pick out the story tonight. What will it be? What's your very most wonderful favorite?"

"*Where the Wild Things Are.*"

His answer stopped Cruz cold.

That had been his favorite book, too. Did most kids love that story or was it a sign that he and Elina's children were connected by more than legal attribution and international law?

You are connected by blood. You are family.

He hurried away to take the call, wishing it wasn't necessary. His work might not seem vital in Grace Haven, a town that boasted the best frozen custard in the state and a sectional championship baseball team, but in Manhattan, people made choices because of moves he engineered on a daily basis. And while his expertise might not seem crucial to a country schoolteacher, it was of vital importance to him.

"I wuv that his supper was still hot," Javier declared when Rory finished the beloved story of a naughty little boy who got sent to bed without supper. "I fink that means his mommy still wuved him."

"Mommies never stop loving their children," she whispered to him. "Here on earth or up in heaven, our mommies love us forever, just the way God wants them to."

"You found us!"

Lily's happy voice made Rory turn.

Cruz was standing in the oak-trimmed doorway, one hand braced against the frame, watching them. He moved forward in an easy fashion, but his face belied his movements. He looked sad, and then Rory realized what he'd heard, that mommies love kids forever.

His face shadowed, or maybe it was a trick of the fading light, but she had the oddest impulse to reach up and smooth his cheek, to caress the anxiety away.

Clearly she was sleep deprived.

He tucked Lily in, teased her a little, then leaned down and kissed her good-night. He didn't hurry the process. It was a kiss that clearly meant something to him, and to the little girl. He turned, grinned at Javier and growled, deep and low. "And now, it is your turn, my little monster!" He crept forward, reciting lines from the book, and Javier sat right up, applauding when he gnashed his terrible teeth, and looking the tiniest bit worried when Cruz began to roar.

Then Cruz sank down on the edge of the twin bed, right next to her. He smelled wonderful, a touch smoky, a little spicy with a hint of some amazingly wonderful aftershave that made her long to move closer.

She resisted the urge and stood instead. "Shall we say prayers?"

"I'm so sweepy," Javier protested, but when he saw Rory's expression, he folded his hands. "But not too sweepy!"

Rory led them through two evening prayers, neither one too long, and when she was done she leaned down to kiss each one good-night.

Cruz didn't move. He sat right there while she smooched Javier and ruffled his hair, and when she was done kissing him, Cruz leaned in and kissed him, too. They said one last good-night, then Cruz followed her out into the hall. Before they were halfway down the stairs, she paused and looked back. "You surprised me in there."

"Because I knew prayers?"

"Not that." She stayed on the second step and faced him. "You kissed them good-night."

"I believe that's customary with small children, isn't it?"

"It is, but you don't have small children, do you?"

He shook his head.

"And I don't expect you do a lot of babysitting in Manhattan."

"No again."

"I just thought it was nice, that's all. You made them smile."

She started back down the stairs to rejoin the others. Five little words made her stop again.

"That's why I did it."

She turned and looked up, and when she did, her heart did that shuffle-step dance once more.

The man was gorgeous. Four steps up he commanded a presence like a Gothic hero, aching from mental and emotional wounds.

"Little kids should always be tucked in. And kissed. And hugged. It should be a law. Or at least a rule."

"I agree."

He descended the stairs separating them. He stopped when he reached her level and faced her, serious. "A long time ago I promised a little boy that if I ever had children, I would be nice to them all the time, no matter what. I would tuck them in and read them stories, buy them ice cream and make their favorite supper as often as they wanted it."

His expression magnified the sincerity of the promise. "Who was the little boy?"

"Me."

She saw it then, what she'd noted upstairs, and in the judge's chambers. A hidden longing for something. Or someone.

He carried his wounds well. Originally she'd thought that Rosa had exaggerated the stories of her time with Cruz, the dreadful mother she'd been. Looking at him, she read the truth in his gaze.

It disappeared quickly, but Rory knew what she saw. A wounded soul and a fractured spirit.

Maybe that's why he did so well in New York, because he pushed himself forward while he shoved pain back.

"Cruz, I—"

He walked past her then, down the stairs and toward the back door. "I'm going to drop in on my mother again tomorrow afternoon. Examine the situation there more closely."

"You've seen her then?"

He didn't look at her. He gazed out over the twilight-lit village. "Briefly. Yes."

"Would you like to take the kids?" Rory asked. She moved closer. "They'd love to see her and they'd be great icebreakers."

"Is it allowed?"

She shrugged. "No one said it wasn't, so let's not ask, okay? She does have a court order to not be alone with the kids, so as long as you're there with them."

"What time shall I pick them up at school?"

"Twelve is good. Unless you'd like to wait until I'm done with my work tomorrow afternoon, and I'll go with you. Provide a buffer."

He winced slightly. "Which means you understand my relationship with my mother quite well."

How much should she say? Rosa had told her things in confidence concerning Cruz, so it wasn't as if he was walking through life, unaware. "Yes."

"It might be good if you were there." He gazed out again, thinking. "I'll come get the kids at noon, anyway. We can spend a few hours together, then we'll pick you up and head out to Casa Blanca when you're done. If you're sure you don't mind."

"I don't mind."

"Good." He turned then, looking at her.

His eyes were dark and somber, nothing like they were during the teasing grin he'd aimed at the children. His expression was drawn and serious, as if he carried the weight of the world on his shoulders. Maybe it felt like that, coming back here. Facing his mother.

He broke the connection and drew open the door. "Good night, Rory. Thanks for letting me come over for supper and to spend time with your family."

"It was nice, Cruz."

He turned just long enough for her to catch that sense of longing one more time. He nodded. "Yes. It was." And then he walked out the door.

Chapter Five

It wasn't Cruz's fancy car that pulled up in front of the White Church the next afternoon. It was Rory's worn and weathered sedan, but somehow the slick financial wizard made the car seem less lackluster. Rory climbed into the passenger seat and tapped the dashboard. "And the current score is car seats—two. Hedge funds manager—zero."

He scowled and the fact that he did it so well showed he'd had his share of practice. "Bested by safety technology." She climbed into the passenger side, laughing. "I expect lack of practice slips in someplace," she teased. "Hey guys." She leaned back over her seat and handed each child a puffed mint. "One each. Do not ask for more, at least until later. Okay?"

"Yes!" Lily unwrapped hers, popped the mint into her mouth, then reached to help her brother.

"I can do it."

She folded her arms, much like Rosa would do. "I was just trying to help. You don't have to be a grumpy pants."

"I'm not a gwumpy pants! Don't call me names!"

Rory cleared her throat. Both kids paused, then got quiet.

"Neat trick." Cruz slid her a quick glance. "Although they've been good up to this point. I barely had to lock anyone up."

"What did you guys do?"

Lily ticked off her fingers. "First we had lunch and Javi had to use the bathroom. Then we took a walk, and then Cruz had to call somebody, so we went to the playground and then he called somebody again, and then we went to visit Mags and took her out and then we came here."

Cruz sent the intelligent five-year-old a cool look of assessment through the rearview mirror. "Clearly my clandestine business calls didn't go unnoticed."

"And yet, they lived." Rory winked at Lily and Javier.

"No lecture?"

"About multitasking? Not from me. Grown-ups have to do it all the time. And I don't believe in hovering over children. That would have driven me crazy as a kid, so I'm going to pay it forward and not be a helicopter parent."

"Helicopter parent? What is that?"

She made a buzzing sound while pretending her right hand was a chopper. "The kind of parent that never lets a kid breathe without them being aware of it."

"There's a name for that?"

She nodded. "There is now."

He looked like he was pondering her words. "You'd agree there are dangers around us, correct?"

"Always have been. Always will be. Part of life."

"I'm kind of amazed." He paused at a stop sign

before heading right to West Lake Road. "I've got a few friends with kids, and they're like that. For all the faults my mother had, maybe it was good that she was so busy building her party business and organizing wine tastings and vineyard weddings, because other than school, I pretty much ran free."

"There were good times?" She kept her voice soft so the children wouldn't hear.

"My father was one of the kindest men ever born. I always knew he loved me and wanted what was best for me, but when neither one of us could please Rosa, it was best to just stay out of her way."

"You're an overcomer."

He made a face. "I don't think of people who come from solid financial circumstances as overcomers, necessarily. I got through, did what I had to do. It worked."

"Why would money matter?"

His quick frown said he didn't understand the question.

"People with money have problems, the same as those without."

"True in theory, but you can buy a lot of comfort if you have the cash to do it."

"But money doesn't buy happiness."

"Maybe not in theory, but in real life?" He raised a brow as Casa Blanca came into sight on his left. "It sure can help."

"We're going to see Mimi!" Lily screeched the words as he turned into the driveway. "I'm so excited! There she is!" She stretched up as far as she could, happy to come back to the only home she remembered, and as soon as Cruz pulled the car into the front loop, she scrambled out of her seat, and out of the car. "Mimi!"

She raced forward and almost barreled Rosa over with a hug of huge proportions. "I'm so very happy to be here, and look who's here, Mimi! It's Cruz, your son. He came from far, far away to help us! Come on, come on!" Lily tugged at Rosa's hand, but Rosa didn't move. She stayed right where she was, her feet planted firm against the wide concrete walk.

Cruz climbed out of the car. He faced her from there. She watched him from her spot, and if Rory hadn't helped Javier out of his seat, she was pretty sure the stubborn duo might have forgotten his presence entirely, but the busy boy broke their standoff by racing to Rosa's side. "Mimi! Hi!"

She bent and hugged him fiercely.

Cruz's hands went tight. His gaze narrowed slightly, almost not enough to notice if she hadn't been watching. Then he relaxed his hands and adopted a nonchalant expression. "I wanted to take some time today to determine the property's value. What's left of it."

The truth of his words cut, because the decline of Casa Blanca had been a town topic for years, but Rosa didn't go ballistic. She glanced around, more hurt than angry, then shrugged. "Some things matter more than others." She palmed each child's head gently. "Life goes on."

Cruz might have to clean out his ears. Had his tough-as-nails mother just intimated that children mattered more than wealth, power and property? Because if she had, he was pretty sure an alien spacecraft had kidnapped the real Rosa Maldonado.

"Cruz, can I show you my room?"

"I want to show him my room first!"

"I asked first!"

"Mimi!"

"Mimi!"

His mother glanced at him, then Rory, then the children, as if assessing the situation. A quick realization hit Cruz.

He had a say in the children's future. His opinion would influence their placement, and his mother realized that.

For the first time ever, he held the power. And it felt good.

"Your rooms are next to each other, so Cruz can see them both." Rory squatted to their level. Both kids got quiet and stopped jumping. "Behave yourselves or I will put you right back in that car and take you to my house where there are chores waiting. If you want to visit with Mimi, be good. Otherwise I pull the plug. Got it?"

"Got it." Lily looked somewhat insulted by the mild scolding, and Cruz glimpsed more of his cousin—and himself, he had to admit—in the girl.

"Yes." Javi looked humbled, as if embarrassed to have been naughty, and that tender nature won Cruz's heart in a totally different way. One needed molding. The other, protection. The shaping of a child was a monumental task, one that should never be taken lightly. Knowing Rosa like he did, a fair man wouldn't risk placing two lost souls into her hands, no matter how she pretended to change.

He let the kids lead him through the side door.

The inside of the gracious party house had fared better than the exterior. As the kids steered him through the household entry, memories swamped him.

Racing down the wide halls with Elina and her brother, Juan. Scaling bannisters and dropping tiny parachuted soldiers from the balcony overlooking the Chardonnay Room. He and Juan used to hide their action figures in the plants around the smaller Cabernet Room, just to see if the housekeeping staff were on their toes.

They were, but every now and again a wedding guest or visiting dignitary would notice the figures peeking out at them and smile.

Rosa hadn't found such things amusing, which was probably why they'd done it.

He followed the children upstairs to the family bedrooms. Javier was in the room he'd shared with Juan when they were small. Lily was in her mother's old room, small, quaint and pretty. The other rooms had belonged to his parents.

As the kids showed him their favorite possessions, he couldn't help but think of his parents. They'd built a business by sacrificing their life together, a business now eroding away. His mother should have taken a lesson from the dinosaurs—that which refuses to adapt will perish, and the family business was close to perishing.

"Hey, guys! Cookies and milk on the veranda!"

Rory's voice made him smile.

Why was that? He wasn't sure, but his response was instant, and he found the reaction confusing.

She was attractive.

He wouldn't have thought he'd be attracted to girl-next-door types, but he was wrong. He *was* attracted, and he was wise to notice that because he had a job to do in Manhattan, and he couldn't afford to be distracted by a woman who lived in Grace Haven. Which meant he'd dismiss the attraction, but as he descended the stairs and spotted her, he realized that would be easier said than done.

She seemed to sense things, and the last thing he wanted was someone assessing his character, because he was pretty sure they'd find it lacking.

As the kids helped themselves to homemade cookies and hugged his mother again, Rory looked on, smiling. Her smile was probably the biggest warning of all. She believed in his mother's apparent change of heart.

He didn't, and because of that, how could he reconcile the thought of leaving two innocent children with a woman who could revert to her old ways in a heartbeat?

He wasn't living in the past. That was a waste of energy. But he learned from the past, and these kids were never going to have to deal with the wrath of Rosa Maldonado.

Rory's phone buzzed with an incoming text from Melanie Carson while Cruz inspected grapevines. The kids were dashing about the property they knew well, laughing and chasing each other in a funny one-on-one game of hide-and-seek, while Rosa stood at the crest of the hill wearing a face of regret. Was it for her lost relationship with her son or for lying about her relationship with these two precious children?

Rory didn't know. She pulled up the text and had to fight a groan when she saw Melanie's message.

Two possibilities so far, both will go fast, both way beyond your price ceiling. Rental is probably the only way to finance the school short-term, then build equity toward long-term projection.

Attached to the text were two images. The first site looked amazing, but so far beyond her budget as to be in another solar system. The second site was way too close to the industrial area near the thruway. Yes, it would be convenient for families going to work in Rochester or Syracuse, but while the building had potential, she hadn't envisioned the hustle and bustle of commuter and tourist traffic buzzing by daily.

She wanted bucolic. Pastoral. A place where kids could run free.

It didn't matter, anyway, because both places were way out of her financial league, with or without the grant money.

What about dividing Belker to buy just the house facing Jackson Road? Were you able to check into that?

The Realtor's return text came back quickly.

Belker seems to be tied up, status uncertain.

Rory stared at the text. Status uncertain? Miss Flora had seemed pretty certain the previous day. She bit back a sigh as she texted back a thank you.

"What's wrong?"

She looked up from the phone, surprised.

Cruz stood near her, looking genuinely concerned.

She made a face and dismissed the text for now. "Not the news I wanted to hear, is all."

"What about?"

She wasn't about to share her plans. To a big-league player from New York, a little kid schoolhouse in the hills would be small potatoes, and she wasn't ready to have anyone scoff at her dream. "A project I'm working on that appears to be over budget."

"Can I help? I'm good with figures."

Oh, she bet he was. No one ran up Wall Street successes without being well schooled in that respect. She might be an upstate woman, but she hadn't been born yesterday. "So am I, and the figures say I need to downsize my plans. Did you find what you were looking for?"

He arched one brow in question.

"In the grapevines. You were checking underneath."

"I was investigating fruit set." When she made a face he went on. "To see how many clusters there were per vine."

"Ah."

He turned, shoved his hands into his pockets and surveyed the sloping vineyard. "My father put his heart and soul into those vines. He had a way of coaxing the grape to its fullest potential, every year. If it was a bad year for Cabernet grapes, he made sure the Rieslings made up for it. It was an art to him." He glanced toward his mother, twenty feet away, but the look in his eyes said it might as well be miles. "She never understood his love for the fields. He never understood her love for pretense and money."

"Leaving you stuck in the middle," Rory said softly.

He shook his head quickly. "I was fine. I found my

way, making my own path between the warring factions."

But it was clear that he wasn't fine, that he'd adapted as best he could in a house divided.

Her parents were strong, faith-filled and loving. They'd set the bar high for relationships for their daughters, and even when they'd lost her older brother, Dave, to a drug dealer's bullet, their faith had helped them through.

Who helped Cruz?

His father gone, his mother distant and the world clamoring for his money-making skills. How easy it must have been to slide into that ego-boosting role.

He glanced back at the phone in her hand. "Sure you don't want to talk about it?"

She shook her head. With so much on her plate this summer, she'd be fortunate to get the paperwork done, much less all her ducks in a row. "Thank you, no. Something I have to iron out for myself."

He frowned instantly. "And I took you away to come here and play peacemaker. I apologize."

Making him feel bad was the last thing she wanted to do when he and his mother seemed steeped in regrets already. "No worries. But I do need to get home and get things set for tomorrow."

"Javi. Elina." He stopped, instantly chagrined that he'd used the wrong name.

Rosa turned.

He raised his gaze to his mother's and she dipped her chin. "It's a mistake I have made often myself. There is such a resemblance."

He almost said something, then didn't.

The kids ran toward him, and Lily frowned, grabbing his hand. "Can't we stay here? Just a little while more?"

Javi looked up, too, his gaze imploring.

Cruz shook his head. "Gotta go. Say goodbye to Mimi."

"Can we come back tomorrow? Please?" Lily wasn't a begging child, but she grasped his hand between hers and Rory wasn't sure if he could resist her plea.

He didn't look down. He looked over her head, at his mother, and then squared his shoulders. "We'll see, okay?"

"But we might, right, Cwuz?" Javi, ever the optimist, grabbed his other hand. "We just might?"

Cruz looked down this time. Two sets of eyes gazed back at him, two hearts, yearning for what so many took for granted: a home. "Maybe," he told them.

They sighed together, relieved.

He hadn't promised, but he hadn't said no, either.

Rory knew kids. These two were sweet and good, but they were also quite normal. He'd said maybe.

And the children would never let him forget it.

Cruz and his mother were caught between a rock and a hard place, Rory mused as she walked into the house an hour later. After seeing Cruz's reaction today, that loomed ominous for all concerned.

"Rory? Is that you?" A very pregnant Kimberly came into the kitchen. "Where are the kids?"

"Cruz is taking them for ice cream."

Kimberly looked at the clock, then the stove. "Was anyone considering making them dinner?"

"You haven't even had the baby yet, and already you're an expert on child care." Rory grinned. "Talk to me when you've managed a classroom of twelve preschoolers with nothing but your wits, construction paper and glue sticks."

"Am I getting bossy?" Kimberly looked sincere, but Rory had been the youngest sister for a long time. She knew better than to say yes, because Kimberly had always been bossy. Rory was pretty sure motherhood wouldn't change that. "You want to be the best mother you can be, and that's understandable."

"In other words, yes, but you won't say so because I might go ballistic."

"And into labor," Rory conceded, "meaning I might have to deliver this baby in Mom's kitchen, and you know how she prides herself on a tidy kitchen."

Kimberly laughed. "Okay, change of subject. How'd it go today?"

Rory pretended to misunderstand. "School was fine, busy and adorable."

"At Rosa's, I mean."

Rory winced. "It was like watching two bulls face off in an arena."

"Did they paw the ground?"

Rory laughed. "They would have if it wasn't concrete. I know I'm a little naive but we had it good here."

"Amazing, actually." Kimberly crossed to the refrigerator and found a box of brownies from Gabby Gallagher's bake shop. She grabbed two, rethought her choice and settled for one, but that didn't mean she wouldn't be back for the second one in half an hour, which is why Rory'd had Gabby pack a dozen.

In the interest of self-preservation, Rory didn't point out that Kimberly had entered the room while munching on a cookie. "I don't know how a parent and child can be that antagonistic toward one another."

"I'm six years older than you are, and I can tell you that Rosa wasn't always a nice person," Kimberly reminded her.

"That's the understatement of the century."

Cruz suddenly appeared at the kitchen door with Mags.

He let the little Yorkie dash inside. "You could just ask me about it, you know." He faced Rory, and she could feel her face flush.

"In fact, we have to talk about it," he continued. "Before any decisions can be made concerning Lily and Javier, we both need to have all the facts. If my mother had her way, she'd let you believe that what you see now is who she is. What she is. But I know different." He splayed his hands, palms out. "You and I need to talk, and we'll need to bring your uncle in on the conversation because he wasn't only our neighbor while I was growing up. He was the closest thing I ever had to a spiritual advisor. I'm pretty sure he won't make me out to be the bad guy because if he felt that way, why would he have called me to come back here?"

"You had a spiritual advisor?" Rory didn't try to mask the surprise in her tone, even though his reference to Uncle Steve made sense. Steve Gallagher would never give power to someone who might abuse it, which meant Cruz's point was well-taken. "Because that's not exactly in evidence now, either."

He stared at the ceiling for several seconds, then dropped his gaze back to hers. Old angst, new anger, loss and sorrow. She read them all, not just in his eyes, but through the body language, the weariness, a full mix of emotions. "I've traveled a long path since my teenage talks with Steve."

"Then perhaps there's a shorter path back," she suggested. "Forgiveness—"

He raised his hand to stave off her words. "We'll talk later. Work has taught me that useless talk is just that. We need Steve on board, and possibly Judge Murdoch, too. So let's wait till then."

Precise. To the point. Obeying the letter of the law.

Rory generally found following rules to be annoying.

Children didn't come with game plans, and in her five years of teaching, she'd learned that broken families often had multiple sharp edges. Smoothing those edges, laying a fresh path for children, was her expertise. Not his.

"Cruz, you want coffee?" Kimberly reached over and tapped the one-cup brewer. "Because you sure do look like you could use a cup. I'll make a tea and we can take it outside and watch little kids dash around the yard and think back to when stuff didn't get so muddled?"

Rory thought he'd blow her off. She thought he'd shrug his shoulders and go his own way, stern and immovable, so when he shot Kimberly a grateful look and said, "I'd like that," Rory was more than a little surprised.

Rosa had revealed a lot about her son, and some about herself, but meeting Cruz—seeing him up close—she realized maybe Rosa's spiel was more self-ingratiating. Maybe she was making herself look less onerous than she'd been.

Which meant Rory couldn't take her current opinion at face value, because on one thing she and Cruz agreed: the safety and well-being of the children was the most important thing of all.

Chapter Six

Grilled cheese and tomato soup. It didn't have to be haute cuisine, it had to be kid-friendly, and it was.

Kimberly had lectured her about the dangers of carb overload, but Rory ignored her and eventually her older sister left with a brand-new book entitled *How to Be an Effective Parent* tucked in her handbag.

Emily had come by with Dolly and Tim, her pre-school twins, and those two little McCarthys ate as much as Lily and Javier did.

By the time Rory got the kids fed, washed and into bed, the idea of tackling the messed-up kitchen after fourteen hours on her feet was not appealing. She walked downstairs, heard Cruz's voice outside and headed to the door. "Did you need me?"

He was watching Mags chase bugs around the yard, thick brown beetles emerging from the ground. "You've got to apply something to this soil or you're going to lose half your veggies and all of your roses and dahlias."

"How's that?"

"Japanese beetles. They're everywhere, and you said your parents were away last year, right?"

"Yes." She nodded and came through the screen door. "Dad was going through cancer treatment in Houston. I know Drew sprayed something for them last summer and it seemed to help."

"Except they managed to live long enough to lay their fertilized eggs in the ground. They've hatched, and now they're going to emerge and quadruple the damage that happened the previous year."

"You had Japanese beetles in your New York garden?" She colored her tone with doubt on purpose, and he laughed.

"At the vineyard. We specialized in grapes, but there was an entire garden maintained to provide fresh vegetables and fruits for the banquet tables for the in-season hosted events. And flowers. Truly magnificent flower gardens. For five months of the year we grew our own produce in the fields and the greenhouse, and that cut down the food budget by fourteen percent."

"That doesn't seem like a lot."

He shrugged. "Take care of the pennies, the dollars will come."

"Ben Franklin?"

He shook his head. "My father. No one knows where the saying came from, but it's true. And fourteen percent is a solid return on investment. What do you make on your savings account?"

She laughed because she hadn't had a savings account, well…ever. "You loved your father."

He sent her a measured look that went beyond her statement.

"Are you trying to psychoanalyze me? If so, please don't. I told you earlier, all you need to do is ask."

"I thought I just did."

He shook his head. "No, you made a statement of assumption hoping I'd corroborate it."

"You are such a negotiator."

He smiled then, and when he did his whole face relaxed. "True enough. Got time to sit? We can talk."

"I've got to load the dishwasher and get it going and straighten up the kitchen."

"I've done plenty of kitchen work in my time. Let's go."

She followed him up the walk. When he stopped and opened the door for her, she didn't walk through. She stood there, knowing they were probably letting bugs in and not caring. "Are you really this nice or is this for my benefit?"

"I'm not known to be nice, I'm known to be tough, but since arriving in Grace Haven, I have noticed an increase in my pleasantries. This could spell disaster for my career. Happily, my associates back in Manhattan will never hear of it, nor will they encounter this side of me."

"What happens upstate, stays upstate."

He grinned at that as the door swung shut behind him. "I guess. You load and I'll wash the stuff that won't fit."

"Because I should have run it this morning and forgot."

"New role, new routine."

He waited until she'd loaded what she could into the dishwasher, then filled the sink with warm, soapy water. When he thrust his hands into the suds, Rory was surprised again. "You've washed dishes before."

"Lots more than I care to admit. I still do most of mine by hand. Not much sense in loading a dishwasher and having a load and a half per week. So I wash and dry."

"Because you love to cook."

"I *like* to cook," he corrected her. "I love to eat. So you and I need to talk, at least a little, because while we're in this together—" he motioned toward the stairs leading up to the kids' bedrooms "—it's a temporary arrangement and we need to be on the same page. First of all, I'd like to set up a schedule to get us through the next few weeks."

"Go on."

He frowned instantly. "You don't like schedules."

"They're necessary, but I refuse to live by the clock."

His hands stayed submerged in the water while he stared at her as if she'd just dropped in from outer space. "Is this where you give me the 'stop and smell the roses' lecture, and if so, can we skip it and move on to how I should appreciate the small things?"

Rory picked up a dish towel and the first clean, wet plate and pointed it toward the back door. "Didn't you just give me a lesson on roses? In light of that, I think you've got the edge on floral care, but when you're dealing with little kids, sometimes you just roll."

"Roll?" He scrubbed the tomato soup pot and didn't look too impressed with tonight's meal.

"Go with the flow."

"I know what it means, but don't children respond better to a sense of order?"

She couldn't disagree with that, but his slightly imperious tone? That wasn't her cup of tea. But he *was* washing dishes so she let it slide. "Consistency is important, but that doesn't necessarily mean living by the clock. I think it's more important to say what you mean so you don't confuse issues."

"No means no."

"Yes."

He smiled and she had to smile, too.

"Keeping it simple and direct works for me," she went on.

"Okay, I get that, and I see your point, but we at least need a care schedule. Will you admit that?"

"Sure. I've got them in the morning, so if you could get your work done then, you could take over in the afternoon so I can tackle the paperwork piling up on my desk."

"If I get them by twelve forty-five, that gives me a seven-hour workday if I hit the desk by five a.m." He nodded, satisfied. "That's doable for the short term, and I can catch up on anything I've missed at night."

"So we share evenings?" She wiped the table down, and when he didn't answer, she glanced up.

Big mistake. Huge. Because when he turned and met her gaze... When his eyes locked with hers, they were right back to that first handshake.

She looked at him.

He looked at her.

Her heartbeat ramped up, then skipped not once, but twice, as if trying to gain her attention. And from Cruz's expression, she was pretty sure he got it, too, but they weren't kids messing around. They were grown-ups, from different walks of life. He'd return to the city in a few weeks and she'd be scouting Craigslist and garage sales for gently used preschool items, their goals at opposite ends of the spectrum.

She dropped her gaze on purpose, then tossed a dishcloth his way. "Can you rinse that out and hang it, please? I'll wash it tomorrow, but it's amazing how quickly a dishcloth can go sour in the summer."

He did as she asked, then drained his wash water and rinsed the sink. When they were done, they faced one another. He glanced up at the clock and made a face. "I can't believe that it's not even nine o'clock and we're calling it a night."

"Not exactly like Manhattan, is it?"

"I'd be sitting down to eat dinner about now."

"Seriously?" As long as he kept his distance and addressed the mundane, she'd be fine around him. "That's a long workday, Cruz."

He crossed the kitchen and dining area, paused at the door, then held out his hand. "Come here."

She hesitated.

He tipped his head slightly. "I won't bite."

She crossed the room and put her hand in his.

He opened the door and led her outside. He didn't pause in the yard beneath the trees. He kept walking until they were in the broad, open expanse leading to Canandaigua Lake. "Look up."

She did, and a star-soaked sky hung over them, stretching down and around in every direction. "Amazing, right?"

He tipped his head back, too, still holding her hand. "There." He whispered the word and pointed slightly east as a meteor streaked across the sky, disappearing into the dark horizon below.

"A meteor!"

He nodded, still gripping her hand. "Yes. My life gets crazy in New York and I don't always remember to go up on the rooftop to see if I can glimpse one or two. The city lights are too bright to see much. My dad and I used to go out onto the top of the hill, with grapevines stretching down both sides, and we'd lie down and watch the meteor showers. The Delta now, Perseids in August. Every year, like clockwork, because that's how the universe is. Balanced and timely. So if I seem to be a little locked to the clock, blame my father."

She heard the smile in his voice and a gentle peace within him, and she could picture father and son, walking uphill to lie back and view the summer sky. "I'm glad you had a good relationship with him, Cruz."

"Great relationship, partially because we needed to create a unified front for whenever Hurricane Rosa went on a rampage. Which was fairly often."

"I think she's better, Cruz. I've only known her personally for a few years, but I've had no problems whatsoever, and it's a rare day I can say that about preschool parents."

He stopped looking up, then he let go of her hand. He rolled his shoulders and shrugged, clearly unconvinced. "We'll see."

He shoved his hands into his pockets and turned back toward the house and garage. "Thanks for going over things with me."

"You're welcome."

It was like a door closed. No more talk of stars or meteors or sweet celestial happenings. They were back to all business, and while Rory knew that was probably for the best, she missed watching the midsummer show with her hand wrapped snugly in his.

Still, it wasn't something her hand—or her heart—could afford to get used to.

Chapter Seven

Cruz's phone jangled him awake an hour before he usually woke up. He spotted Drew's name and swiped the screen swiftly. "What's wrong?"

"Your mother."

A thick knot formed in Cruz's throat. "Tell me."

"She called 911 and was transported to Rochester Regional Hospital. They've got a great cardiac facility there, and her doctor's affiliated. That's all I know."

Cruz was accustomed to shutting his emotions down to focus on business, but his cool head abandoned him this time. "I'll head right in."

He had the sudden urge to call Rory and tell her what was happening, but should he call at this hour? Drew saved him.

"I'll call Rory in an hour or so. We'll know more then. No sense waking the kids so early."

That was sensible. Why call her now, in the middle of the night? Although he wanted to, just to know he had her support. Drew was right, though. He grabbed clothes from the small closet as he finished up the call. "I'm on my way. Thanks, Drew."

The GPS app on his phone guided him into the ER parking lot about thirty minutes later, a long drive for an emergency situation. He exited the car and jogged into the ER receiving area. "My mother was just brought in by Grace Haven Volunteer Ambulance. Rosa Maldonado."

"Two East." She pointed down the hall alongside the ER waiting area. "Show your ID to the guard, go through the doors and follow the line to the red elevators."

Following her instructions, he arrived on the second floor, only to be stymied by more locked doors and an intercom system.

Had it been like this when his father got sick? Had he lain behind locked doors with no one to visit him because Cruz had been too busy in New York to comprehend the gravity of his illness?

Guilt rose like a tidal wave.

He pressed the intercom button, answered the nurse's questions and when she instructed him to have a seat in the small adjacent waiting area, he bit back a retort.

He didn't want to wait.

He didn't do waiting well, another Rosa characteristic. He wanted answers and he wanted them now.

"I expect a cup of coffee sounds pretty good."

He turned quickly. Steve Gallagher held out a steaming cup of coffee that smelled as good as anything he could buy in New York City. "I won't deny how happy I am to see you. Did Mom call you?"

Steve shook his head. "Tara saw the ambulance lights and woke me up. She likes to run around the lakeshore before work, and she was up in time to see the ambulance pull away. I called Drew and he filled me in. You okay?"

Cruz gripped the heavy-duty paper cup tightly and glanced around. "This is where my father was, too, right?"

Steve nodded. Cruz didn't mention that he'd never made it home to see his father before he died.

"Did she visit when he was here? My father, I mean? Did she come to see him?"

Steve held his gaze. "No."

Remorse hit him hard. "I didn't, either," Cruz confessed. "I knew he was sick, she'd called me, and I was going to come up that weekend, and then he was gone. Just…" He drew in a deep breath, then blew it out. "Gone."

"No one expected him to die, Cruz."

"But when I was sick, he took care of me." His fingers curled into his palms and stayed there, tight. "When I was hurt, he was always there for me. When I needed stitches, he hopped into the front seat of that farm truck and drove me to the ER so fast, I was sure we'd get a ticket. And when he needed me, I was too busy wrapping up business to fly up and sit with him. He must have hated me, Steve. And who could blame him?"

There. He'd said it. He'd voiced what he'd been feeling all these years. What his mother had thrown at him after the lackluster funeral she'd thrown together for a wonderful man.

"He loved you."

Cruz scoffed.

Steve took a sip of his own coffee and sat back. "Think what you will, but I was here with him every single day, and all he ever talked about was you. How proud he was. How thrilled he was with your success. How he loved America, because where else could an uneducated immigrant marry a landowner's daughter, have an incredible son and do the job he loved all of his days? He may not have had the best marriage…"

That caught Cruz's attention. He looked up, curious.

"But he had the best life because God had blessed him with verdant fields, a chance to give back to so many and a perfect son."

Cruz wasn't perfect. He wasn't anywhere close to good, much less perfect, but in his father's eyes…

He closed his eyes and imagined Hector Maldonado looking down at him like he used to, the gap-toothed grin, the brindled beard that had turned gray, the sun-weathered skin a deep copper brown. "Do you think there's a heaven, Steve?"

"I know there is."

"And I'll see him again?"

"The Lord giveth. The Lord taketh away. Blessed be the name of the Lord."

Why was it so much harder for an educated man to grasp the innocence of belief than an uneducated man like his father? He'd believed freely, all his life. He'd come north to seek freedom, and to embrace faith, hope and love, and once here, he'd encouraged his sister and her children to do the same.

The children.

A chance to give back to so many…

Cruz understood those words. Hector had helped Elina's mother and her children. He'd sent money back to Mexico, to help fund immigration and education, despite Rosa's scolding.

The double doors opened. A woman strode in wearing a white coat. "Mr. Maldonado?"

A wealth of feelings rose up inside as he studied her grim expression. "Yes?"

"It's not good news."

He'd read that in her eyes. "How bad is it?"

"Her heart has suffered considerable damage. I can't give you a real prognosis, but she's in a compromised state with minimal hope of recovery. At some point her heart will give out one more time, and she'll be gone."

He turned to his former neighbor and mentor. "Steve, I'm going in. Can you call Rory and have her bring the kids?" He turned back to the doctor. "We have two small children in Grace Haven, children she was raising. It's all right if they come to see her, isn't it?"

"It is. And when you've seen her, we'll need to make some decisions, Mr. Maldonado. Whether to keep her here in the hospital or put her in a nursing home."

"Home."

She misunderstood him and nodded. "I'll look into available beds."

He shook his head and gestured toward the window. "No, not *a* home. Her home. We can hire nurses to give her care, and if she's going to die, I'd like her to pass away looking out over the fields she loved, in the home she was raised in. Can you have someone look into that for me? If we're going to lose her, I want it to be on her terms."

"We could be talking days, not weeks," the doctor explained. "Or you could get everything arranged, and she might not survive the trip home."

That was a risk he had to take. "No matter what

happens, at least we'll have tried. If you can get her stable…"

"Exactly what we're working on now."

"Then we'd like to bring her home. One last time."

He held her gaze and she obliged. "I'll have the hospital social worker take care of it as soon as she arrives."

He walked into his mother's room in the northeast corner of the cardiac care unit. The morning sun had broken the horizon, and Rosa's window looked out over a checkerboard of fields and farms.

The head of her bed was raised. The soft clicks and whirs of machines kept track of her vitals while oxygen eased her breathing. "Mom?"

Her eyelids fluttered closed, then opened. She saw him and sighed.

"You gave us a scare."

She didn't look at him. She gazed down and her free hand picked at the woven cotton blanket.

"How are you feeling?" He wasn't used to making small talk with his mother. "Are you in pain? Can I get you anything?"

Again she picked at the blanket, then paused. "Another chance."

She whispered the request so softly, he had to lean in and ask her to repeat it. "What did you say?"

Eyes down, she fingered the cotton again, then raised tired eyes to his. "Another chance, Crusberto. With my son. My only son. The love of my life."

He stared at her.

Never had she said such words to him. Never had she intimated that he mattered. Yes, she'd worked hard and long, tirelessly, trying to build her formal event empire. She'd raised the bar for other venues, and she'd brought a lot of business to the area. But she'd never implied that her devotion was to anything but money.

Remorse rose again, because wasn't he following a similar path?

He sank onto the edge of the bed and took her hand. "Your heart's been damaged."

She grimaced. "They told me this is the last time, that I might not make it through the next spell."

So she knew. "The doctor is very nice."

She nodded.

"She suggested that they either keep you here or in a nursing home, but I want to bring you home. To Casa Blanca. To hire help to take care of you." He paused because he wasn't accustomed to asking permission to make decisions, but this time it seemed right. "Is that all right with you?"

"To come home? Until—"

"Until whatever the good Lord's got planned comes to pass, I'd say." Steve walked into the room. He leaned down and gave Rosa the gentlest of hugs. "You like the idea, Rosa?"

"Yes," she whispered again, and her fingers knit the cotton fabric more fiercely. "I want to come home."

"Rory and Corinne are bringing the kids in to see you for just a moment," Steve cautioned. When she began to thank him, he motioned to Cruz. "His idea. Not mine. And then we'll work with the hospital to get everything set up for you at home."

"Yes."

Cruz began to rise, but she reached out and caught hold of his hand and a corner of his heart, as well. "Will you stay? Please?"

His mother, asking him to stay. Asking him to share her time. Saying she cared…

Of course he'd stay. He sank back down onto the chair and held her hand. He wasn't sure when Steve left. He might have dozed off, he might have been remembering old times, old friends, deep green grape leaves and thick, juicy clusters of fruit. He only knew that when Rory and her sister-in-law slipped into the room with Lily and Javi, he felt more at peace than he had in a long time.

Lily seemed to assess the situation quickly. "Mimi is very sick, isn't she?"

"I am." Rosa opened her eyes. She found Lily in Corinne's arms and smiled. "But I am so glad to see my sweet ones. Have you been good?"

Lily nodded.

Javi scrambled into Cruz's lap and grinned at his ailing caretaker. "Mimi, I have so much to tell you! I saw a book wif fwee dinosaurs fighting! They were not big in the book, but Cruz said that in real life they were so big, they were big like buildings! Can you even believe it, Mimi?"

Love softened her gaze as she looked at the small boy. Joy brought a hint of smile to her mouth. "I can't, Javi. I can imagine it, but I can't imagine seeing it. But you, my darlings." She raised her left hand slightly. "You will see so much. Do so much. And Cruz will make sure you have every chance there is to love your family, your faith and your freedom."

He knew what she was asking. She wanted him to ensure that the children would be kept safe in America, safe with him. There was no way in the world he could refuse that request. "I'll make sure."

She sank back against the pillow, relieved. Her eyes drifted shut.

Rory touched Javi's shoulder. "We've got to go now, honey. Mimi needs sleep."

"I'll follow you out." Cruz stood, holding Javi against him, and when they made it to the automated door, he handed the boy over to Rory. "I'm bringing her home, Rory. For whatever time she has left, I'm bringing her home."

"I think that's a wonderful idea, Cruz."

It was, but what a shame it took a life-and-death matter for him to see the perils of holding grudges versus the grace of forgiveness. "Overdue, but…" He shrugged. "I'm going to get things lined up with Steve's help, and I'd like to get the place back in shape for her. So she can see it like it was, before everything fell apart. If I can manage quiet workers."

"I'm quiet!"

Javi made the declaration in a voice that was anything but quiet.

"Shh." Rory motioned to the door. "I'm going to get these sweet things out of here. We can talk later, or Uncle Steve can fill me in."

"I know it puts extra weight on your shoulders." Cruz didn't want to mention the responsibility of the kids. Rory's expression indicated she understood.

"Well, we're Gallaghers, and we've got big shoulders." She bumped her forehead gently to Javi's, teasing. "We've got this, Cruz. You take care of your mom, and we'll pray. I'd love for her to have enough time to see your plans for Casa Blanca."

"Me, too."

They left with the children, but as they approached the bank of red elevators, Lily looked back.

Sorrow filled her gaze. In five short years she'd known too much loss. Too much change.

He couldn't let them go to strangers, but how would they adapt to life in the city? His work hours weren't kid-friendly. He'd have to hire a live-in nanny to watch over them, but was that in their best interests or his?

He couldn't worry about that now. Right now he needed to make sure things were put in order for his mother's return home. Anything after that would have to wait, because Cruz had made a pledge to make a difference at Casa Blanca, and it was going to take a lot of hands-on effort to see it got done.

He texted Chen a brief message to oversee his workload for the day, then called his boss. Rodney Randolph hadn't developed one of the nation's biggest investment firms by being easygoing. He wasn't going to like Cruz's news, and there was no way of knowing how the man would deal with it, but with Rosa's condition and his guardianship of the children, Cruz had no choice.

Chapter Eight

Rory had just gotten home from the preschool class with the kids when her cell phone rang with a call from Kimberly over at Kate & Company. She left the kids with their next-door neighbor and raced through three neighbors' yards, four driveways and across the paved lot leading to the rear entrance of the event center. "Kimberly!"

"In here." Her sister's assistant poked her head around the corner from the front entry. "But not for long," Allison added cheerfully as Rory hurried her way. "I've called Drew, he's on his way, and it appears we're having a baby."

They couldn't. Not today when there was already no one around to help with anything... Rosa was so sick. And Cruz was tied up at the Rochester hospital.

"You can't have this baby now." Rory stooped low and faced her older sister. "It's absolutely, positively the worst possible time, Kimberly."

"Sensible or not, the baby's coming. And so is Drew," Allison said, making a face as the sound of a police siren squealed toward the traffic light at Main

Street and Route 20. "That siren's got your name written all over it, darling."

"No siren." Kimberly puffed out a breath of easier air, then grabbed Rory's arm. "Call him and tell him no siren or I won't go. I'll have this baby right here in my office."

She meant it, and when Kimberly laid down the law, it was a pretty sure thing that it would be followed. Rory hit Drew's number in her phone. "Kill the siren, Drew. If you don't, I promise you the end result won't be pretty."

He laughed.

"Is he laughing? Is that him laughing?" Kimberly reached for the phone, but fortunately another contraction pulled her attention away from husbands and sirens.

He pulled up to the door—without the siren—about thirty seconds later. In less than two minutes he had Kimberly in the car, and they were on their way to the hospital.

Rory sank into one of the striped, upholstered chairs. "Tell me that didn't just happen."

Allison made a face that said it did.

Emily strode in, waving her phone. "Janet's got the bridal shop, I'll cover here, and, Rory, who's got the kids?"

Janet was Emily's top salesperson at the bridal shop. She'd worked there for years before Emily bought the store, so the bridal shop was in good hands. "The kids are with Mrs. Wyatt, next door. Cruz is with Rosa at the hospital, Tee Tee has gymnastics class tonight, and Callan and Amy have a league game in Victor. I promised someone would deliver Amy to the hospital once the game was over." Corinne's son, Callan, played hardball for the town team, and Drew's daughter, Amy, had won a spot on the team, as well.

Allison raised her hand. "I'm free to help with whatever you need. If Corinne gets the kids to the game, I'll pick up Tee and meet them at the ballpark when her lesson is done. That way Corrine can bring her kids back home afterward and I can drive Amy into the hospital to meet her baby brother or sister. With Janet on bridal store detail, you and Emily can go to the hospital to greet the baby while Grant watches the twins."

"You go." Rory faced Emily. "I've got to watch Lily and Javi. I can't hand them off no matter how much I'd like to be there. They've had enough crazy going on in their lives. I hate to miss the excitement, but honestly, the baby won't know if I meet him or her on day one or day three."

"You sure?"

"Positive. What hospital needs that many Gallaghers at once?"

"Good point." Allison winked. "Hey, if you bring Lily and Javi to the baseball game, they can cheer on the team and have a quick supper at the park."

At least that would be easy. And taking Javi and Lily to the baseball game would keep their minds occupied while Cruz worked to get Rosa's situation settled. Of course it meant no work on the grant again, but... She breathed deeply, pushing angst aside.

Children should always come first. Work would have to wait.

Rory's text came through as Cruz was leaving the hospital shortly after nine that evening.

It's a boy! David Andrew Slade, born at 8:57 p.m., 7 lb. 10 oz. All is well, we're celebrating the happy occasion here at home!

He called her right back, chagrined. She'd been so excited about this new baby, and what it would mean to their family. "You missed your sister's baby being born? Rory, I'm so sorry, you should have called me. I'd have come back there straightaway."

Her quick reply eased his guilt. "This baby is going to be here for a long, long time. I will hold him, laugh with him, teach him funny things and rock him to sleep. I've got time, Cruz." Her voice softened, and in that gentleness he felt her compassion. Her concern. "You don't. I'll see little Dave, and I'm pretty sure he's not going to care if it's today, tomorrow or the day when they bring him home. I'll be here, waiting."

"You're not upset?"

"Not in the least."

"But I expect you'd like to go see him."

"Not at this hour." She laughed softly. "Let's see what tomorrow brings, okay? My guess is our little Dave is going to look pretty much the same tomorrow as he did today."

He wasn't used to this kind of reaction. She wasn't casual about the baby's birth, he recognized the joy in her voice, but she handled things with a peace and contentment he didn't quite understand, but admired. "You've had the kids all day, and you've probably been run ragged."

"It's been busy," she admitted. "But we're doing all right. How was Rosa when you left her?"

"Resting comfortably, and if we can get everything ready at the house, we can bring her home in two days."

"That would be wonderful, Cruz."

He felt that way, too, as long as being around him didn't rile his mother up too much. Today she'd welcomed his time, his presence, but Cruz wasn't sure if she'd feel quite that magnanimous when the medications were reduced. He hoped so. "I'm taking charge of the kids in the morning. You sleep in. I'll come over and do breakfast and all the other stuff you pretend is so easy."

"That's silly, I—"

"It's not silly. It's a way of saying thank you for going the distance, Rory. I couldn't have done this today without you, or any of the other days. And I know you're balancing on your own tightrope, too, so let me do this. Please."

There was a moment of silence before she agreed. "All right. I would actually love an extra hour of sleep. Javi's an early riser, and Lily's a night owl, so by the time she's actually asleep and I can go to bed, we've gotten pretty deep into the evening."

"Perfect." He was glad to find a way to help her, something that wasn't financial. She might be low on funds, but she didn't value money like so many he knew. She valued time and self-sacrifice.

Was he trying to impress her? When he knew he was leaving eventually?

Maybe. He wasn't sure. He knew that he liked to make her smile, that she was amazing with the kids and she was a calming presence around his mother.

Yes, he was leaving. He had no choice; his work was in the city. And she'd be staying here, following her own dreams.

As he took the thruway exit toward Grace Haven, the thought of uprooting Lily and Javi concerned him. Kids needed love, strength and continuity, didn't they? Something solid?

Rory would add faith to the list, and the longer he stayed in Grace Haven, the more relevant that seemed. If he assessed family, love and unity the way he did investment bundles, the faith element clearly made a difference. How could an intangible have such an impact?

A text came in. He glanced down at the traffic light east of the toll and sighed.

Presence required in office. Crucial negotiations, sensitive data. Return tomorrow as originally planned.

Cruz turned off the phone.

Rodney would be angry, but he lived his life angry, so that was nothing new. He wouldn't understand a dying mother and two orphaned children. No, he'd understand…he just wouldn't care.

A week ago, Cruz would have had a similar reaction. Not now.

He'd worked for years to attain this level of prestige. He was on the verge of being one of the best movers and shakers in the financial district. A bad move now could bring it all crashing down.

But until things were settled here, he needed to remain.

Until his mother was gone.

The truth in that scared him, because for the first

time in decades, he cared about his mother. No matter what Rodney threatened from his fiftieth-floor office…

Cruz wasn't going to leave his mother to die alone.

Cruz rarely set an alarm to wake himself in the mornings. He was a creature of habit, up late and up early, but tonight was different. He had two kids counting on him, and he'd promised Rory a chance to sleep late. He wasn't sure why that seemed so important, but it did so he set his phone alarm, just in case.

But he never heard it. Either that, or it never went off, so when he awoke thirty minutes after he was supposed to, panic set in.

Cruz never panicked.

Today was the exception. He threw on clothes, skipped the shower and raced to the Gallagher house. He let himself in and listened…

Blessed quiet surrounded him, so the kids hadn't woken up and disturbed Rory yet. He put a coffee pod in the brewer and pushed the button.

Nothing.

He stared, realized someone had turned the brewer off and fought back a growl.

He never turned his brewer off. He was a New Yorker, and he was pretty sure turning the power off could be construed as un-American. He hit the power switch to warm the water, then tiptoed up the stairs to wake the kids.

"A mornin', Cwuz!" Javi jumped straight up in the bed as if he was part jack-in-the-box. "A morning!"

"Good morning to you, too, little man." He put a

finger to his lips and lifted the boy out of the bed. "Can you tiptoe downstairs?"

"Sure!"

Clearly the kid didn't know the meaning of the word because it sounded more like a small elephant dashing down the hall, then the stairs. He'd made it to the living room below when he hollered, "I found my cwothes!"

Cruz grimaced. So much for letting Rory sleep late.

He went to the second bed and put a hand on Lily's shoulder.

She shrugged him off and rolled over.

He did it again and was pretty sure she growled.

"Lily. Time to get up."

Her eyes blinked open, she saw him and squawked loud and long.

"Hey, it's me, Cruz, I'm taking you to breakfast this morning. Wake up, sleepyhead."

She stared at him hard as if trying to make sense of the situation. He expected her to grumble and want to curl back up to sleep.

The last thing he expected was what she said next. "I didn't want him to hurt my mommy."

Cruz's heart paused. His hands went still. He stared at the innocent five-year-old in front of him, and couldn't find words.

"I told him not to. I told him again and again, but he wouldn't listen to me."

What could he say? What should he do? Was it good for kids to remember bad things?

He sank down on the edge of her twin-size bed. "Were you little?"

She nodded. Her lower lip stuck out and her chin

trembled. "Real little. And my mommy kept saying, 'Hush, baby, hush. It will be all right. Don't you cry.'" She wrapped her arms around a threadbare bunny and held Cruz's gaze. "But it wasn't all right, and Mommy cried and cried and so did I."

Devastation rose inside Cruz.

What had this child witnessed? What had she been privy to as a tiny little girl at the mercy of heartless people? "Did he hurt you, honey?"

She shook her head and Cruz released a breath he didn't know he'd been holding. "I'm sorry, Lily."

He didn't know what else to say. He didn't know how to offer comfort, how to erase bad memories. But he did know how to hold a little kid to help them feel safe now, so he gathered her into his arms on the edge of that bed and snuggled her close.

Her hair smelled like sweet cherries. Her cheek was pressed against his shoulder, and her heart thumped hard against her chest.

She'd lived in fear. She'd witnessed something horrible. And as he sat there offering the scant comfort he could, he knew he and his mother would agree on one thing: these children would not be going back across the border.

He'd do whatever was needed to keep them here. No matter what.

A movement in the doorway drew his attention. Rory stood there, her arms crossed around her middle, her expression dark, and when his eyes met hers, he knew she'd heard.

She recovered first. She pasted a smile on her face, stifled a yawn and said, "Good morning, sweet pea!

Cruz, if you don't mind, I'd love to come to breakfast with you guys. Is that all right?"

"Yes," he answered quickly, because she'd just thrown him a lifeline, and only a stupid man would refuse it. "I'd like that, Rory. Are Lily's clothes downstairs?"

"On the sofa, and from the sounds of it, Javier's dressed and ready to go. I, on the other hand, need ten minutes. And coffee."

"I'll take care of both." He stood, still cradling Lily. "Come on, kid, I'm giving you a ride downstairs on the Cruz Maldonado shuttle."

"Okay."

One word, so soft, almost unheard.

He passed Rory in the doorway. She laid her soft hand against Lily's cheek, then leaned in and brushed the girl's face with butterfly kisses. *"Que todas las bendiciones de Dios sean el suyo el día de hoy y los que vendrán, mi preciosa."*

She was wishing blessings on a precious child, all the days of her life. Cruz smiled at Rory as she straightened and stepped back. *"Ciertamente el Señor te ha dado un espíritu de lucha."*

It is certain that God has given you a fighting spirit. He spoke the phrase as a compliment. Rory Gallagher had a gentle side, but her expression indicated she was battle-ready to fight for these children. He respected that.

Her smile said she appreciated his understanding and his reply. "Not everyone sees the fighting side of me, Cruz, but then I only fight as needed. When it comes to God's little ones…" She lifted her eyes from Lily to meet his. "I take off the gloves."

FREE Merchandise is 'in the Cards' for you!

Dear Reader,

We're giving away FREE MERCHANDISE!

Seriously, we'd like to reward you for reading this novel by giving you **FREE MERCHANDISE** worth over $20 retail. And no purchase is necessary!

You see the Jack of Hearts sticker above? Paste that sticker in the box on the Free Merchandise Voucher inside. Return the Voucher today… and we'll send you Free Merchandise!

Thanks again for reading one of our novels—and enjoy your Free Merchandise with our compliments!

Pam Powers

Pam Powers

P.S. Look inside to see what Free Merchandise is **"in the cards"** for you!

We'd like to send you two free books like the one you are enjoying now. Your two books have a combined cover price of over $10 retail, but they are yours to keep absolutely FREE! We'll even send you 2 wonderful surprise gifts. You can't lose!

REMEMBER: Your Free Merchandise, consisting of **2 Free Books** and **2 Free Gifts**, is worth over $20 retail! No purchase is necessary, so please send for your Free Merchandise today.

Get TWO FREE GIFTS!
We'll also send you 2 wonderful FREE GIFTS (worth about $10 retail), in addition to your 2 Free books!

Visit us at:
www.ReaderService.com

Books received may not be as shown.

YOUR FREE MERCHANDISE INCLUDES...

2 FREE Books **AND** 2 FREE Mystery Gifts

FREE MERCHANDISE VOUCHER

2 FREE
BOOKS
and
2 FREE
GIFTS

Please send my Free Merchandise, consisting of
2 Free Books and **2 Free Mystery Gifts**.
I understand that I am under no obligation to buy
anything, as explained on the back of this card.

❏ I prefer the regular-print edition   ❏ I prefer the larger-print edition
105/305 IDL GLTL   122/322 IDL GLTL

Please Print

FIRST NAME

LAST NAME

ADDRESS

APT.#   CITY

STATE/PROV.   ZIP/POSTAL CODE

Offer limited to one per household and not applicable to series that subscriber is currently receiving.
Your Privacy—The Reader Service is committed to protecting your privacy. Our Privacy Policy is available online at www.ReaderService.com or upon request from the Reader Service. We make a portion of our mailing list available to reputable third parties that offer products we believe may interest you. If you prefer that we not exchange your name with third parties, or if you wish to clarify or modify your communication preferences, please visit us at www.ReaderService.com/consumerchoice or write to us at Reader Service Preference Service, P.O. Box 9062, Buffalo, NY 14240-9062. Include your complete name and address.

NO PURCHASE NECESSARY!

LI-517-FMIVY17

► Detach card and mail today. No stamp needed. ►

© 2016 HARLEQUIN ENTERPRISES LIMITED   Printed in the U.S.A.

READER SERVICE—Here's how it works:

Accepting your 2 free Love Inspired® Romance books and 2 free gifts (gifts valued at approximately $10.00 retail) places you under no obligation to buy anything. You may keep the books and gifts and return the shipping statement marked "cancel." If you do not cancel, about a month later we'll send you 6 additional books and bill you just $5.24 for the regular-print edition or $5.74 each for the larger-print edition in the U.S. or $5.74 each for the regular-print edition or $6.24 each for the larger-print edition in Canada. That is a savings of at least 13% off the cover price. It's quite a bargain! Shipping and handling is just 50¢ per book in the U.S. and 75¢ per book in Canada.* You may cancel at any time, but if you choose to continue, every month we'll send you 6 more books, which you may either purchase at the discount price plus shipping and handling or return to us and cancel your subscription. *Terms and prices subject to change without notice. Prices do not include applicable taxes. Sales tax applicable in N.Y. Canadian residents will be charged applicable taxes. Offer not valid in Quebec. Books received may not be as shown. All orders subject to approval. Credit or debit balances in a customer's account(s) may be offset by any other outstanding balance owed by or to the customer. Please allow 4 to 6 weeks for delivery. Offer available while quantities last.

BUSINESS REPLY MAIL
FIRST-CLASS MAIL   PERMIT NO. 717   BUFFALO, NY

POSTAGE WILL BE PAID BY ADDRESSEE

READER SERVICE
PO BOX 1341
BUFFALO NY 14240-8571

NO POSTAGE
NECESSARY
IF MAILED
IN THE
UNITED STATES

◄ If offer card is missing write to: Reader Service, P.O. Box 1341, Buffalo, NY 14240-8531 or visit www.ReaderService.com ►

He'd thought her sweet and kind, and she was both, but right now, gazing into Rory Gallagher's eyes, he didn't see the innocent kindergarten teacher he'd happened to meet.

He saw a warrior, more like him than he'd have thought possible.

"I'll meet you guys downstairs."

"Yes."

He took Lily down and set her on the couch. Javier launched instantly into stories about last evening's ball game and how he didn't like to eat breakfast right away.

His chattering seemed to help Lily. She smiled at him, got herself dressed, then joined Cruz in the kitchen. She'd brushed off the dream, or the surprise of waking to see Cruz in her room.

He couldn't.

Her face and words had shocked him, but he shouldn't have been shocked. He should have been forewarned and on guard. He knew that Elina's brother had succumbed to the promise of cartel money. He knew that his aunt had liked flaunting rules, a quality she'd encouraged in her children.

And look what it got them. Both gone.

"I'm sorry I was scared of you this morning." Lily came to his side and slipped her hand into his. "I wasn't really scared of you. I was scared of the dream *and* you."

He knew what she meant, that waking up and seeing him had melded too well with her nightmare.

"It's all right." He pressed his lips to her forehead, determined to help her heal and hope. "It's all right, honey."

"I bet Sadie's got blueberry pancakes this morning." Rory kind of sang the words as she came into the bright, open kitchen wearing a sundress that made him wish summer would last forever. "With whipped cream. And yes, Javier my friend, you may have yours to go and eat it later at snack time."

The kid grinned like someone had just handed him a bag of candy. "Fank you, Rory!"

"You're welcome. Are we ready?" She looked at Cruz, and he had to hand it to her. She did all this way better than he did.

"We are."

"Let's do this."

Outside they started to cross the drive to cut through The Square, but Cruz made them stop. "Hang on. I forgot something." He took the stairs two at a time, grabbed his electronic notebook, stuffed the charger into his pocket and trotted back downstairs.

Rory noted the electronic tablet with a glance. "Getting a little work done with your pancakes this morning?"

"No, ma'am." When she looked puzzled he tapped the carrying case. "Early-morning box score updates."

"Nice." When she directed a full-on smile his way, he was pretty sure the sun shone brighter and the air smelled sweeter.

He held Javier's hand in one of his and the tablet in the other. "I concur."

He held the door open when they got there. Rory let the kids go first, then followed them. He followed her, and when he did, three pairs of eyes watched them from the middle booth.

"Did he bring it, Badge?" Jim Reilly's poorly disguised whisper crossed the nearly empty eatery.

Badge looked disappointed. "Nope."

The kids scrambled into the booth opposite the three old-timers while Sadie waved from behind the well-washed counter.

"Say hey to the cutest bunch of early-mornin' regulars I could possibly want! Mornin', y'all! How are we today?"

"Fine." Rory beamed at Lily, then Sadie, as if everything was normal and nice. Cruz determined that he would follow her lead and they could discuss things later, away from little ears. "We'd love coffee if you've got some to spare, and chocolate milk for my friends."

"I'll get that right away, and I hear congratulations are in order for the new chief of police and the Gallagher clan. A baby boy!" Sadie's vibrant tone indicated she thought babies were the best things ever. "I can't wait to see him, Rory."

"I should have known word would be out. The police force is worse than a bunch of old hens when it comes to gossip." She started to sit as Cruz set his tablet onto the men's table. He tapped a few things, then slid it toward the back of the table. "Here's your Major League Baseball updates, gentlemen."

"You brung it?" Tyler Brown looked happy and surprised. "It's a different thing, ain't it? It looks different."

"Smaller, easier to carry."

"Hey, did you see that?" Badge poked Jim as a highlight touted a late-night catch by Mike Trout. "It ain't half human for a body to leap that high, is it?"

"It's somethin', sure 'nuff." Tyler reached over and

shook Cruz's hand. "Thanks for totin' it along. It makes the mornin' real special."

"No problem." He slid into the booth next to Javier. "Something smells wonderful, Sadie."

"Well, now." Sadie rested the coffee carafe on the table and her other hand on her hip as she faced him. "I see we are beginnin' to settle in if we're startin' to appreciate the smell of home cooking." She poured his coffee and Rory's, then hooked a thumb toward the kitchen. "Sal's got a batch of well-done home fries, all mixed up with fresh chopped sweet onion, green peppers and parsley straight out of Tyler's garden."

Tyler almost blushed for all his seventy-plus years.

"No one grows sweet peppers or nicer critters than they do at Brown's, just like no one used to be able to rival a spread like your mom and dad put on, Cruz, back in the day. They had a routine that bested just about every other place on the shore, do you remember that?"

He did, and usually the memory was accompanied by a nasty stab to the gut, but when Sadie brought it up, it sounded nice. "I do."

"They made quite a team," she went on as she pulled out her order pad. "When you worked at Casa Blanca, it was like a well-oiled machine from start to finish. At least it was back then," she added, because it was pretty obvious the well-oiled machine had long since corroded.

"Did you work there, Sadie?"

She jutted her chin toward Lily and Javier. "I was waitstaff there when you and Elina jumped from hay bales to annoy goats and chickens. But then I got mar-

ried and had a few kids, and those late nights for weddings were hard. Gus took over the diner from his
daddy and they needed help. Still, it was a pleasure to
see those fancy parties. I learned a lot, watching your
mama, and I still use a lot of that knowledge today."

He didn't remember Sadie, but he and Elina weren't
inside much in the early days. "Please tell me I was
nice to you," he said once they'd given their order, and
she laughed.

"You were a beautiful, busy little boy and your
daddy doted on everything you did. There was many
a time when your mama had to track him down because he went off playing with you kids. They were
happy back then, but busy. Maybe too busy."

She went back to the kitchen.

Cruz didn't look at Rory. He knew she was studying
him, analyzing Sadie's words. He didn't need analy-
sis, but right now he wasn't 100 percent sure what he
did need.

His phone signaled an incoming message. He lifted
the phone, scanned Chen's text and stood. "I'll be right
back."

Rory had set up tic-tac-toe boards on the back of
the kids' placemats. "We'll be right here."

He walked outside and placed the call quickly.
"Chen, what's up?"

"Problems in Asian markets. Our price for Hobaku
just went up. Way up."

"Counter, Chen. You know what to do."

Chen sounded less certain. "They're used to dealing
with you. When I talk to them, they act insulted, as if
they're getting the junior varsity squad. And Rodney's

due back soon. He's already all over me via text as if I'm a fresh-off-the-street know-nothing."

When Rodney Randolph got agitated, he spewed venom. It hadn't happened in a while, partially because of the upmarket, but mostly because Cruz had been quite successful in setting up bundles and assets that made a rich man richer. "He's mad at me, not you. You just happen to be in the line of fire, and I'm sorry about that. And with hedge fund values slipping, he's on the rampage, although the man is richer than any group of ten would ever need to be."

"It's making things tough here." Chen wasn't one to pretend. "But we'll deal, Cruz. One way or another. Rodney's threats just add a whole new level of discomfort to an already unpleasant situation."

Cruz paced the sidewalk, agitated. Rodney was using Cruz's absence to be a jerk. He loved control, and didn't like initiative unless it was to bank megabucks into the coffers, and while Chen was a Harvard Business School graduate, he didn't have Cruz's years of experience and Rodney wasn't above feeding the younger man to the sharks.

Breathe… Think… You're upset by what Lily revealed. Don't let it affect business. Separate the two.

The reminder helped. "Play hardball. Walk away. Let them take the hit."

"And if we lose them?" Chen's voice squeaked slightly, as if he couldn't quite believe what he'd heard.

"We gain the next one. Set the tone and the rules, Chen. Calm, cool and professional. They know there's more fish in the sea. So do we. Report back later, but

I'm tied up after three. On the personal side, were you able to cut the deal for the Belker offerings?"

"Done. I contacted the local Realtor on the down low, offered fair value. She texted me acceptance. I contacted Washburn right away, and found out they've had Grace Haven on their priority list for years, but finding commercially zoned land big enough for development has been a problem. You've made them very happy, and you'll get a significant profit."

"I appreciate you handling that."

"That's what friends do, Cruz."

"Thanks, Chen."

"Glad to help. Who's the p.m. conference with? Bennington Harvester?"

"No." He'd be contacting the international agricultural equipment company midmorning to talk about a potential takeover. "This afternoon I'm spending time with my mother. Like a normal person would."

"How's she doing?"

Funny. He and Chen never talked family at work. It was an unwritten rule to leave real life at the curb when you took that elevator ride. Because they dealt with sensitive matters and potentially stock-changing information, they couldn't make calls or go online from the firm, except for chosen account avenues. For Chen to ask seemed nice—and out of place. "She's dying."

"Cruz." Chen paused and sighed. "I'm sorry, man."

So was Cruz. "I appreciate it. Keep me informed about Hobaku."

"Will do."

He walked back inside, torn.

His colleagues were taking a mental and verbal

smackdown because their boss was angry with him. It was a cowardly bullying tactic that shouldn't be allowed.

He slid back into the booth.

Rory eyed him, concerned. He made a face and shrugged. He hadn't realized how much two adults could say without words until he'd had to do it around kids.

"I'm heading to the hospital from here. Steve's going to be on hand when the medical equipment is dropped off at Casa Blanca later today. Mrs. Reichert has agreed to do the daytime shifts, and we've got a health-care aide coming in evenings. Once we have her back at the farm, I'd like the kids there as often as possible. I'll be there with them the whole time," he added, because Rosa was still under a court order to not be alone with the kids. "I think it would be good for everyone."

"I love being with my Mimi." Javi slurped his chocolate milk through his straw. "Will she make me cookies with sprinkles? I wuv sprinkles so much, Cwuz!"

"She doesn't feel good, Javi." Lily frowned at him. "She's sick and you can't make cookies when you're sick."

"Well, maybe Cwuz can make them? I'll help!" Ever the optimist, Javi turned innocent eyes his way.

Rory chimed in. "I'm the cookie maker around here, and maybe we can make some when I'm done with school. I think Cruz is going to be busy trying to fix things at Mimi's house, but summer preschool ends soon, and then there will be more time."

"Are fings broken?" Wide-eyed, Javi looked from her to Cruz. "I didn't fink fings were bwoken, Cwuz."

"A few things," he told the boy, frankly amazed

at how endearing a little kid could be. Who knew? "Nothing I can't fix."

"I bet you can fix everything, Cruz." Lily's look of confidence restored order to his frenetic, Manhattan-based world. "Mimi says you know everything."

Rory suddenly tapped her watch. "Guys, we've got to hit the road."

"I'll drive you all to school."

She shook her head. "The walk does us good. We talk about things, we pray, we thank God for flowers…"

"And sunshine!" Javi fist-pumped the air.

"And squirrels and birds and candy." Lily giggled when she added to the last. "Miss Rory loves candy so much."

Cruz stood. The children were trapped between them, but he was still close enough to catch the scents of sweet vanilla soap and coffee. They went well together, but he was beginning to realize that most things went well together when Rory was around. "Sweet tooth?"

She frowned. "Terrible. Short women should be born with an allergy to carbs. Unfortunately, that's not the case."

She made him smile.

He couldn't remember the last time he felt this comfortable around a woman, not needing to impress them. With Rory, his wealth and standing were more likely to put her off than attract her, which was oddly refreshing. "Then I'll walk you."

She looked up.

He gazed down, and for the life of him, he didn't

want to break eye contact with her, but when Sadie handed him the check, he had to.

Tyler lifted the electronic notebook. "Cruz, don't forget your thing."

Cruz reached into his pocket and pulled out a charger, then handed it to Sadie. "Sadie, can we keep this one here for the guys to use in the mornings? I'm going to be busy at my mother's for a while, and I'm not sure how often I'll get in here first thing."

"I'd be happy to oblige." She took the charger and tucked it behind the counter. "That way you boys will be ready to go every morning over coffee."

"That's sure nice of you," said Badge.

"Real nice!" added Tyler. "Thanks, Cruz."

Their combined smiles helped dispel Rodney's mean-spirited tactics, but Cruz knew he'd have to deal with his boss eventually, and probably sooner rather than later. "Glad to do it, boys."

As the group of them walked up Main Street toward the White Church, the urge to hold Rory's hand seized him.

He couldn't, of course. Except it seemed like the right thing to do, and he almost did it when their fingers brushed, but they brushed because Rory was pointing to the opposite side of the road. "There's my dream, right there, up for sale at the perfect time as long as I get my grant application written and approved."

He followed the direction of her hand and stopped in his tracks. "What?"

"The Belker buildings. Not all of them, of course, but the old house in back there, facing Jackson Road. It's the perfect location for a day school."

"What is a day school?"

"A combined preschool and kindergarten. My goal is to begin one for disadvantaged kids. That way low-income families would have access to pre-K and start school totally prepared for success."

What were the chances that they'd both be looking at the very same piece of property in the town? "Why there?"

"If they divide the parcel, I think I can get the house at a decent price. That way I can build equity while the school gets off the ground."

There had to be other locations for a preschool, but as he was thinking, they came to the hand-lettered sign pointing to the rear of the White Church and he realized maybe there weren't a lot of other places. He also knew that a hotel or inn needed adequate parking, so cutting off a piece of the property wasn't possible. With no parking square footage, the value of the property would nose-dive considerably. "Have you thought of building a school?"

She made a crazy face. "If I get my grant written, and if they allow me the financing to start the school, I'll be fortunate to be able to manage the down payment and upgrades on the Belker house. The grant doesn't give the kind of money I'd need to build from the ground up. And besides, I like the idea of a quaint house, a yard, a more homelike feeling. No, that's my dream, right there." She looked back down the road and smiled, and her smile just about crushed his heart in his chest. "Miss Flora Belker is looking into things for me. I talked with her the other day. If it's meant to happen, it will happen."

He didn't know what to say. She already thought

he was money-crazy. What would she think when she found out about him buying a chunk of land on the spot just to resell it to a higher bidder and walk away with a significant profit?

He knew what she'd think, and it wasn't anything good.

"I'll keep the kids today so you can stay with Rosa, and then tomorrow I'll drop them off at the farm to stay with you. That way they keep up on their lessons, and you have time to get work done. Cruz, you know that fixing up Casa Blanca is a huge undertaking, don't you?"

Oh, he knew that, all right.

Plus he realized he was quite possibly ruining her dream, her school for disadvantaged kids. What kind of person did that?

Lily hugged him tight, then Javi jumped into his arms, wanting a hug, and when he set him down, what he wanted to do was to pull Rory into his arms, too, and hug her goodbye. To thank her for the example she set and the warmth she effused, and the black-and-yellow sundress wasn't anything a smart man shrugged off, either.

She smiled at the kids, then tipped that same smile up to him. "Give our love to Rosa, all right?"

Keep it simple. Uninvolved. Because when she realizes what you've done, she'll most likely kill you.

He stepped back. "I will. I'll call if there's any change."

"Of course."

She took the kids' hands and headed up the church driveway, unaware that he'd swept her property out from under her under a proxy name.

She'd think he'd done it to hide, and he had, in a

way, but only so the price wouldn't go up. Which didn't make him feel like any less of a scoundrel.

He walked back to the Gallagher house, got into his car and headed north to the hospital just outside Rochester. He'd figure this out, somehow, but right now he had to do something he'd never done before. He had to swallow his pride and put his mother first. Then he'd tackle the rest.

Chapter Nine

When Rory made the turn into Casa Blanca that afternoon, Javi sighed out loud. "I just wuv this pwace so much." His voice took on a dreamlike tone, which was partially because he did love the big grape farm, but also because he was a little boy who simply wanted to go home.

"I know, little man, and that's why we're here. Cruz is meeting us and I do believe he's bringing fried chicken."

"I don't like bones!" Lily looked like she'd prefer death to bones, with little room for discussion.

"Me eever," declared her little brother. "Mimi never makes us eat chicken wif bones. Not ever ever."

She should have told Cruz to get nuggets. Didn't most kids love chicken nuggets? Why didn't she tell Cruz to get the boneless bites kids love?

He pulled into the drive as Regina Reichert came through the front door with Uncle Steve. The kids dashed up to see Regina, their nearest neighbor before Brian Gallagher's farm up the road, and Rory intercepted Cruz as he stepped out of the car. "Please say you got nuggets."

"What?" He stepped out, looking downright puzzled, then smiled when he understood the question. "I did, actually, because the gal at the window said most kids prefer nuggets and I'm all about making kids happy these days."

She grabbed his arm. "I'm so glad! The kids were about to mutiny over the thought of eating bones."

"How can there be anyone who doesn't love fried chicken?"

"I can't even."

He laughed, and then he slung an arm around her shoulders as if it belonged there...or as if they were long-lost friends, which they weren't. "I love the way you talk."

She paused and made him pause, too. "As opposed to the way Manhattan women talk?"

He didn't answer, and when he walked up the steps with her, he removed his arm from her shoulders to shake Regina's hand. "Thank you for coming on board with this, Mrs. Reichert."

"I was happy to do it, but call me Regina, okay?" she told him. "Since I lost my husband, life's been a circle of I-don't-know-whats, spinning here and there, so taking care of your mother will help ease me back into a workforce I left a long time ago. She'll get the best care I can give, Cruz."

"I have no doubt." He raised the take-out bags. "There's plenty of food. I'd love for you to stay."

Steve bowed out. "I've got to get home to do premarital counseling for a betrothed couple, but I expect eating alone gets old, doesn't it, Regina?"

"It does, and I'd love to stay. But only if you're sure."

"Positive and honored," Cruz told her, and the sincerity in his words made the older woman smile.

He had a knack, maybe one that hadn't been used too often in his line of work. Or maybe it had, and Rory was fooling herself about his sincerity. Certainly she felt somewhat naive in his company, but that could be the dollar signs shrieking from his designer clothes.

The kids wolfed their food down like starving pups, then begged to go to the creek.

Regina took one hand in each of hers. "I'll walk them down while you clean up."

"Deal." The kids convinced her to go through the overgrown vineyard, and the tug of vines made for slow going, but by the time the kitchen was put to rights, their joyous voices rang out from the slow-flowing creek. "Sounds like they found the water, all right."

"It does." Cruz opened the door, waited for her to pass through, then closed it. "Let's go see some fish."

"Yes."

She started forward.

He reached out and caught her hand. "Come this way. Let's not fight the vines." He led her to a double-wide space separating two kinds of grapes, still holding her hand.

He could have let go, but he didn't, and when they came to the more level ground and the thin creek leading to Canandaigua Lake, he squeezed her fingers lightly.

Her heart did a flip-flop before she scolded it into submission. There was to be no falling for the rich guy going back to New York, and that was that. He lived a life she hated, with a money-is-everything mind-set.

The kids dashed in and out of the cool, meandering stream, screeching and laughing. She focused on their innocence and joy. This was the kind of thing she embraced. Hometown goodness, family fun.

A splash of fresh, cold water in her face made her suck in a breath. She screeched and swiped her sleeve on her face to dry it.

And then she met Cruz's gaze.

He was laughing at her from a crouched position below. He splashed her again and she laughed with him. "So it's war, is it?" She dashed into the shallow water and paddled water toward him with both hands. "You can take the boy out of the country, but you can't take the country out of the boy."

Regina backed away, hands up. "I'll let you guys have your water fight while I head home. Cruz, I'll be here tomorrow morning, first thing."

"Thank you, Mrs.—" She scolded him with a look. "Regina. Thank you, Regina."

"You're welcome."

Within minutes they were soaked. The kids raced around, scaring fish and frogs and whatever else might have been sunning in the shallow waters.

"I'm so wet!" Lily held her arms out, laughing and dripping from every inch of her hemmed dress. "I am the wettest person ever!"

"I believe you are." Cruz palmed her head with a gentle touch. He smiled down at her. Lily looked up at him and smiled back, and that silhouetted image made something crystal clear for Rory.

Cruz should raise these children. It was right there

before her in the two winning smiles, the warm emotions that passed from man to child.

"I'm soaked, too!" Javi raced out of the water and shook himself as hard as he could, spraying droplets in a full circle. "Hey, wook! I'm a puppy! Woof! Woof!" He started chasing Lily up and down the narrowed rows between the grapes. She pretended to be a cat, so their combined voices mewed and barked from side to side.

"They'll dry off faster than we will," Cruz remarked as he started up the nearest row. "Shall we try running through the grapes to speed the process?"

She laughed as the kids darted in front of them again. "No, I just realized I'm winded from dancing in the creek. That means I better start jogging again. Or swimming. Or something non-sedentary."

"How about one-on-one basketball in the driveway after the kids are in bed?"

She scoffed at the challenge. "Of course you'd pick that. The height difference alone would make you the clear winner."

"I'll only use one hand. It's a shame to waste that hoop, Rory."

"Except you appear to be ambidextrous, so I still claim a disadvantage."

He laughed, and it sounded so nice to hear him laugh like that. She hoped he found it pleasant, too, that he liked it enough to find more to laugh about in life. "All right, I'll spot you five points."

She rolled her eyes. "Make it ten and you've got a game."

He held up a hand for a high five. "Ten it is."

* * *

Rory Gallagher had fast feet and could bank a three-pointer like no other woman he'd ever known.

He'd given her a gratuitous ten-point lead to be nice, but as she fought—and fought hard—to hold the four-point lead she still maintained, Cruz had to hand it to her.

She played well, and played to win, which meant he'd better stop underestimating the petite woman or she'd be holding the upper hand in hoops, and who knew what else she had up her sleeve?

She dodged right, went left and curled in under, faked a layup and stepped back to bank a backboard shot.

Was it adrenaline? Competitiveness? Being flat-out stupid?

Cruz wasn't sure, but when that ball made a perfect arc toward the basket, he rose up, extended his arm and blocked the shot hard, bouncing that ball off Rory's face.

Her nose began bleeding instantly.

She grabbed the hem of her T-shirt and brought it up to staunch the flow, but Cruz had dealt with basketball gushers before. He pulled his outer shirt off the bench, thrust it into her hands and said, "Here. Use this." She accepted the wadded cotton and pressed it to her face while he ran to the kitchen for paper towels and ice.

What had he done?

He'd hurt her.

He'd gotten caught up like the supercompetitive jerk he was and smacked that ball into her beautiful face.

Her nose...

He cringed, remembering, and rushed back out of the house. She'd taken a seat on the nearby garden bench. He slid in next to her, handed her a paper towel ice pack and dry paper towels for the nosebleed.

"Thanks." She accepted both without yelling at him, scolding him or giving him a dirty look. She let his shirt fall to the ground and replaced it with the folded paper towels. "Obviously you've had nosebleeds before."

"I played hoops in college. Elbows and balls to the face were a given. Listen, Rory, I'm sorry, I—"

She scowled, not listening. "I had the perfect arc on that ball. Did you see it?"

"Well, yes—"

"I was that close to pulling back to a six-point lead and wham!"

"I know, about that…"

"One of the best blocks I've seen in a while. Cruz, you had great vertical, and you're already tall, so that was impressive."

He paused, looking at her more closely. "Did I miss the part where you wanted to kill me?"

"Because you blocked my shot?"

"Because I knocked you in the face with a basketball. And I'm big and you're not big."

"Yeah, but I had a ten-point differential. And I had no intention of losing," she assured him. She pulled the toweling back. "I think it's stopped, but I'm going to let the ice hang out for a while. Have they developed treatments for a broken nose yet?" she wondered out loud, her head tipped back, then answered her own question while his heart tried to stop beating. "No, it will probably just need reconstructive surgery once the bones heal. And who has time for that?"

Guilt wasn't just rising inside him, it was erupting like a Pacific Rim volcano, ready to blow—until he saw her smile.

"Gotcha."

She smiled with her head tilted back, keeping the ice on the left side of her face while the thick maple leaves rustled above them. "How is it?" He leaned forward to examine her face.

Her very beautiful face.

"Better," she whispered, glancing at his eyes, then his mouth. "Much better."

"Rory." He cupped a hand to her cheek. Soft. So soft. And not delicate like he'd supposed a few days before. Talk about looks being deceiving. He started to lean in, thinking how wonderful it would be to kiss those sweet lips, but Mags started going little-dog crazy. She darted across the yard, back and forth, yapping up a storm. She danced on two back legs, yapped again, then danced some more.

A car pulled into the driveway. It rolled right up to the far side of the garage, backed into the turnaround and parked.

Rory jumped up, excited.

The dog was plenty excited, too, leaping and barking, spinning in circles until the car's occupants climbed out.

"Mom! Dad! You're home!" Rory ran across the drive and hugged both of them. "This is the best surprise! Everyone's going to be so excited to see you!"

"Well, we heard there was a new baby, and a couple of cute kids staying at the house, and thought you guys might be able to use some extra hands on deck!" Kate

Gallagher laughed in delight. "How on earth could we stay away?"

"Cruz?" Pete Gallagher crossed the driveway. Cruz met him halfway. "Rory said you got called back here to help with Rosa's problems, and I want you to know right off that we're happy to do whatever it takes to help you and your mother."

Cruz couldn't have heard right. Could he? "Excuse me, sir?"

"With the vineyard and Casa Blanca. We've had our share of problems these past two years, but your parents were instrumental in helping Kate get her event-planning business off the ground thirty years ago. We owe them, and now that I'm feeling well again, we're going to jump in and help you get things back in order. Once we get settled and see this new grandson—"

"Little Dave!" Kate Gallagher sang out the name in her excitement.

"—we can sit down and make a plan. I tend to work better with a plan, don't you?"

Cruz did work better with a plan, but the thought of others wanting to help hadn't occurred to him. Why would they? "I'd be happy to work with you, sir. Possibly ecstatic, as a matter of fact."

"Good! Good!" Only then did the man notice the blood on Cruz's T-shirt. "Son, you're bleeding. Let's get you inside."

"He's not, I am." Rory raised her hand. "Bloody nose, Dad, no biggie. Let's head in, but remember the golden rule you taught me." She blocked their way and lifted a hand. "If you wake the kids, you take care of the kids."

Kate laughed, then clapped a hand over her mouth.

"We won't. I promise! Oh, it's so good to be home again!"

"It sure is." Pete started to follow them into the house, then turned. "Are you coming in?"

Cruz shook his head. "Not this time. I'm going to grab a shower, jack up the AC and call it a night. Nice to see you again, sir."

"You, too. It's been too long." Pete started back toward the house, then turned again. "She's got fast feet and a tough three-point arc, doesn't she?"

He meant Rory, of course.

She had all that and more, and he'd been about to kiss her and would gladly take that opportunity when the chance came again, but he felt weird hoping for that in front of her father. "She took me by surprise." Talk about an understatement. "Good night, sir. And welcome home."

"You, too!"

He'd heard that phrase several times since he'd come back. Each time he heard it he wanted to argue the status, but after nearly kissing Rory?

The term *welcome home* didn't feel quite so foreign, after all.

Chapter Ten

Coffee and cinnamon teased Rory's senses the next morning. She rolled over in bed, sure she was dreaming, then sat straight up, delighted. Her parents had come home, which meant food…and maybe a return to normal.

She hurried downstairs, grabbed her mother in a hug and twirled her around the kitchen. "I am so glad you're back."

"Me, too." Kate kept her arm around Rory, and swept the kitchen a fond look. "Right now it seems like we've been away forever, and I needed to come home. Help you girls. Hold that baby. And your father agreed."

"It wasn't like there was much choice in the matter." Pete came in through the screen door and stretched. "I was hoping to see Cruz this morning, but he must still be sleeping."

"No, he's been up for a while," Rory assured him. "Try the diner. He's been going over in the morning, sharing box scores with the guys."

"I'll walk over." He kissed Kate, then Rory, and walked out the door, whistling softly.

"He looks good, Mom."

"He is good," Kate assured her. "I was worried after the treatments, but he's bounced back wonderfully. If I'm not careful he's going to regret his retirement and want to get back on the job."

"Bouncing a new baby on his knee and following Callan and Amy on the baseball circuit will take up some of his time. And is he serious about offering to help at Casa Blanca? Because I'm sure Cruz would love it."

"Very serious." Kate's voice firmed. "Rosa had her faults, but her ambition helped develop a steady base of clientele for Kate & Company and many others in the Finger Lakes. We can't ignore her in her hour of need. I'm sorry it's gotten this bad, but with some hometown help, I expect we can help her turn things around."

"I don't know if it's that easy," Rory started, but two overhead thumps meant two small children were about to join them. "But I'm happy to help, too."

The kids raced down the stairs, turned into the kitchen and stopped. They stared at Kate, then Rory, and gulped at about the same time.

"Guys, come here. This is my mom. Her name is Kate and she's come back home to help us with things. Mom, this is Lily and Javier Maldonado."

"Good morning to both of you."

Lily shrugged into Rory's side and said nothing.

Javi took Rory's hand and stared up at Kate, then turned his attention to Rory. "It's nice that your mommy came back, Miss Wory."

Such heartfelt words from a little fellow whose mother would never come back. Kate winced, then bent low and pointed to the table. "I made some special cinnamon rolls for you. I need taste testers. Do you know what those are?"

Both children shook their heads.

"They're people who eat special foods and tell us if they're good. Can I count on you two to do that for me?"

Javi took her quite seriously and nodded. "I fink I can! But what if I don't wike it? But maybe I will," he added quickly so he wouldn't cause offense.

"Oh, you darling, thank you for being brave. And if you don't like it," Kate added, "you don't have to eat it. We can start with a tiny piece for you to test. Okay?"

"Okay! Come on, Wiwwy!"

Lily moved forward with more caution, but one bite of the warm frosted cinnamon rolls won her over. "These are so good, Miss Kate! I think they're like the best I ever had!"

"Well, good, I'm glad you like them." Kate poured two small glasses of milk and set them on the table in front of them, then faced Rory. "I called Emily, and I'm meeting her at the office once you guys are off to school. I want to help while Kimberly is out with the baby, but I don't want it to look like I'm taking over."

"This is Emily we're talking about," Rory reminded her. "She won't let you step on her toes, and she'll love the help because we were trying to set up a workable schedule for August and kept coming up with blank spots. Mom, this is perfect timing."

"Speaking of perfect timing, I couldn't help but notice the interesting proximity of Cruz Maldonado to my youngest daughter when we pulled into the driveway last night."

Rory was not about to go there, not yet, anyway.

She hadn't had a minute to figure this out herself, so talking about it with her mother was off the table. "He felt bad about my nose, which is actually still kind of tender." She felt her nose gingerly. "But it doesn't appear to be broken, so if I lay off contact sports for a few days, I should be fine. He does have a solid vertical, though."

"He looked pretty solid all around," Kate deadpanned, then turned toward the door when a car pulled into the yard. "There's Emily now, and she's brought the twins to see their grandma!" She rushed out the door, and between Dolly and Timmy screeching, Mags's yapping and the women's voices, Rory was transported back to a time when her whole family was here, laughing, living and working together.

She hadn't known how blessed she'd been. But then her friend Millicent had come over to play one day, and she'd looked around the house, the yard, the assorted family and friends inside and out, and whispered, *I wish I could live here, Rory.*

Rory hadn't realized the true meaning. She'd laughed it off and said, *But your mom would miss you, silly!*

A few years later she understood. And she discovered how foolish teenage choices could go on to haunt you for a long time to come.

The twins rushed to the door. She swung it open and hugged one, then the other, and as Timmy started jabbering to Javier, the two little boys giggled and laughed. Lily watched more seriously. Dolly had to work harder to climb up onto a chair, but when she finally made it, the special needs little girl's face shone with pride.

Rory couldn't go back and change the past. She

knew that. But she could make a difference in the future and maybe that would atone for being a stuck-up twit all those years ago.

Rosa was home.

Regina had ensured that everything was in place in the Cabernet Room, and Cruz made sure Rosa's bed faced the broad west windows, overlooking the vineyards. Pete Gallagher was coming to help capture and trim the vines after he met his new grandson. Rory was bringing the kids over, and Cruz was making a list of what needed to be done.

The list was huge, and he'd gotten about halfway done when his phone rang. His boss's private number appeared in the display. He let it go for three rings before he answered. "Rodney, good morning."

"Where are you, Cruz? Because I know you're not at your desk, which is where I told you to be."

"I explained, sir. My mother is terminally ill and I'm helping her get things in order. And spending time with her. Chen is—"

Rodney exploded. He didn't like to be disobeyed, and Cruz had refused to come back to the office, which meant the never-satisfied boss already had a full head of steam worked up. "Don't tell me about Chen! He's an incapable youngster who has already blown one deal and is seriously undermining the next one, which puts him precariously close to being terminated because I don't lose easily, Cruz. You know it. I know it. I need you back here now. I didn't hire you to work remotely, I hired you to be on-site, and that contractual position has not changed. You either get back to the office or you're fired."

In Cruz's world, the best didn't get fired, they negotiated terms with other movers and shakers and changed offices. To be let go smacked of ineptitude and Rodney knew it, which was probably why he was using the threat.

So be it.

He'd always planned to leave the firm on his own time frame. That didn't seem possible unless the boss was bluffing, but right now, Cruz didn't care. "Feel free to send me the termination of contract via email."

He hung up.

He thought he'd feel bad.

He didn't.

He felt as if something had changed, but not necessarily for the worse.

No job, but money in the bank and time to set things right in Grace Haven.

Rory would call it God's will. His timing.

Was there such a thing? He'd come back here testy and angry. He'd surveyed the downfall of his father's industry, and his mother's bad choices.

He should feel terrible, but he didn't and he wasn't sure how to rationalize any of it, except that maybe the man he was today was different from the guy who'd purposely rolled into town in a luxury car.

He pocketed the phone and stepped into the lower barn. The upper barn was where they'd stored equipment, with a section for the dairy goats to dash in and out as needed.

He almost looked that way, as if "Mama" and "Mia" would lead the rest of the goat herd across the fenced-in area, looking for food.

Brian Gallagher's mother used to create old-style cheeses for his family, and goat milk fudge.

Three Mennonite farms had supplied custom cuts of meat and eggs for Rosa's specialty dishes. And the Bach farm had provided fresh lamb, perfect for Greek wedding feasts.

He paused outside the barn, examining the past through adult eyes and wondering if he'd uncovered a truth he'd never seen. Choreographing all of this and utilizing it in a successful business didn't just take hard work, it took vision. His mother's vision.

The barn smelled old. He found the smell offensive, an insult to Hector's memory. He opened the three south-facing windows, letting fresh lake air flood the interior. The movement was just enough to cut through the stale scent.

He took down a whetstone and the hand scythes, then descended to the creek. He sharpened the blades old-style, like Hector had done for decades, using the cool creek water and the dark gray stone to hone the perfect edge. And when the noise of children drew his attention up, it was Rory he saw, standing there. She'd shaded her eyes with her hand, searching for him, and when he stood, their eyes met.

Would she come down? Or should he move forward?

He moved to take a step when a text buzzed in. It was Chen, with one single word.

Fired.

He wanted to swear.

But he didn't, and when the kids dashed through

the overreaching strands of grapevine, he was glad of his restraint. "Hey, guys! Rory brought you over?"

"And we can stay! I'm so 'cited!" Javi leaped into his arms and Lily grabbed his legs, but their reaction drove the point home. Chen had a wife and two kids. Sure, he'd find another job, but just as good? As well paying? And was it Cruz's fault that his work partner was getting the boot from an angry boss? How could he manage what he needed to do here with Chen's fate on his shoulders? Maybe that was Rodney's plan. To fire Chen to force Cruz's hand, to make him come back. He and Chen had worked together for a while. They'd built a team. Rodney knew that.

He set Javi down while he texted Chen back.

Strong-arm tactic, will call later.

He got back three short words.

Was escorted out.

Leave it to Rodney to add embarrassment to the equation. To lead Chen out as if he'd done something wrong, a man who erred on the right side of legalities every single time there was a choice, even if Rodney would have preferred otherwise.

"Can we have lunch, Cruz?" Lily asked. She added a little tug to his arm for effect.

"I'm starvin'!" Bug-eyed, Javi gazed right into his face, and there was no doubting the intensity of his little-boy look or his hunger.

He'd never thought of lunch for the kids, which meant he might have to start making lists to remember all the little things that went into having children to care for. "Sure. Let's go see Rory and Mimi."

"Miss Wory had to weave." Javi's shoulders drooped and his chin aimed down. "She had to get stuff."

"I wanted her to stay with us." Lily clutched his hand tighter. "She makes me smile all the time, and I don't worry about things when she's with me."

He felt the same way. Things took on a brighter perspective when she was around.

"At least she's coming back." Lily let go of his hand and skipped ahead. "But her dad is here, and he's going to help."

Lily's words made him smile, despite the news from New York.

"Cruz." Pete was hailing him from two rows over. Cruz crested the top of the vineyard and moved that way.

"Rory went to buy scrapers to start working on the front of the house."

"To start painting?" He'd figured on hiring a team to come in and take care of the scraping and painting, but there hadn't been time to do that yet.

"Yes. I told her white satin, top quality, and half a dozen scrapers and brushes. And a couple of small buckets for when folks are on ladders. I thought you might want to pick the shutter colors, but that's easy enough once the base paint is finished.

"Kate's visiting with Rosa right now," he went on, "and Regina's daughter came over to keep an eye on the kids while her mother keeps an eye on your mother."

His surprise must have shown because Pete clapped him on the back. "Cruz, you've been in the city too long. That's how it's done here. At least once your mother let down that wall of pride she spent years erecting. You ready?" Pete aimed a look his way, and Cruz nodded.

"Yes, sir, I am."

"Well, let's send these youngsters inside for lunch and get a move on."

Rory pulled into the Casa Blanca driveway, got out of the car and whistled as she crossed to the edge of the hill overlooking the trellised slope. "I can't believe the difference ninety minutes has made. The vines look so much better. And the tangle is gone on these two rows."

Her father slapped Cruz on the shoulder. "This guy knows his way around a vineyard. But then, he was taught by the best."

"Dad had a way with the vines." A mix of pride and sadness tinged Cruz's tone. "I didn't know I still remembered all of that, honestly."

"And yet, you did." Pete's tone offered praise for a job well done.

Rory turned his way. "And you're feeling all right, Dad?"

"They operated on my brain, not my arm," Pete teased, and when she looked chagrined, he laughed. "It feels good to be doing something again. Don't repeat this to your mother, at least not yet, anyway, but I was sick to death of traveling from place to place, seeing things. Once I started feeling better, I knew I'd much rather be *doing*. Watching other people do things gets old real quick, so I'm glad to be helping out here. I'm happy to be feeling better and to be home."

He gave Rory a half hug, then moved toward the

house. "Mom ordered pizza for six o'clock, then we're getting cleaned up to go visit that new grandson again. And I'll be back, first thing in the morning, Cruz."

"I'll welcome the help, sir." He watched Pete stride into the back entry of the house, then looked down. "He's amazing."

Rory nodded. "We like him pretty well."

"He doesn't talk much."

"No. But when he does, we listen. And Mom talks enough for both of them, so it's all about balance. I can't believe these first rows look this much better. It's amazing, Cruz."

"You think?"

She looked up at him, and when he tipped his gaze down, she couldn't think at all.

He took her down the first row and when he demonstrated how they captured the vine, then trimmed and tucked it back into the wire fencing, she whistled softly again. "How did you know to do this? The vines look so much better and I can see the grape clusters now. They look positively happy."

He laughed softly. "I think they are. They love the sun. My father truly enjoyed all of this." He gazed across the vineyard rows. "He grew up working for my grandparents. My grandfather taught him everything. And when they died, they left everything to my mother, but she'd never worked the field. She knew nothing about the farm production side of things."

"And yet she made this place into an amazing event center," Rory observed. "How?"

"That one's easy." He ran a hand across the nape of his neck as his gaze swept the broad, sprawling farm. "She worked, night and day. She saw pictures in magazines and she wanted Casa Blanca to be like those pictures."

"It worked."

"She'd gone to college, gotten a degree in interior design and used some of that to decorate the reception areas, but new businesses struggle. Hers was no different, and she knew nothing about how to have one business offset the other."

"But your father did."

"He wasn't a citizen. But if they married, he'd become one and she'd have expert help bringing the vineyard to fruition."

"A marriage of convenience?"

"Except he loved her." His voice deepened. "It was there, in everything he did, in everything he said, for so long, but it was as if she was ashamed of him. And maybe of me, by default."

"She's proud of you, Cruz." She moved in and took hold of his arm. "She told me all about you. She's told lots of people in town about her wonderful son, his great successes. As if raising you was something she did right while all of this was eroding around her. Did you ever think that maybe neither of you really understood the other? And that maybe you should have talked more?"

"Talk more?" He made a face. "Effort was encouraged. Talk was barely tolerated."

"Which means the three of you walked around with your feelings bottled up, exactly what I tell kids not to do. Sometimes dealing with grown-ups is a whole lot more confusing than the simple honesty of children."

"A lesson that's clearly working with those two." Cruz pointed toward the nearby barn. "Lily's not afraid to speak her mind, and Javi's always trying to make people happy."

"Beautiful, diverse personalities. Like God intended us to be." She followed the direction of his hand, leaned against a vineyard post and smiled, and when she did, a shift of wind swirled her hair across her cheeks, her face.

She reached up to push the hair back.

Cruz beat her to it. His big, strong, beautiful hand swept the hair back behind her ear, then stayed right there, holding her cheek.

Perfect.

The feel of his hand to her face, his roughened palm against the softness of her skin.

She looked up into his eyes. Serious eyes, deep and richly toned.

His focus shifted to her mouth, wondering.

He didn't ask permission and she didn't want him to. It was as if this moment was scripted long before they'd met.

And when he drew her closer and deepened the kiss, her heart beat in time with his. "Cruz…" She whispered his name as he held her close to his chest.

"Best kiss ever." He whispered the words, making her smile. "I've been thinking about this for a while, Rory."

"You haven't been in town all that long," she whispered back.

He laughed softly. "That should tell us something. If it seems like too long to wait, it probably is."

"Cwuz!" Javi spotted his hero and ran their way. "Cwuz, I saw the b-b-biggest fish!"

"This big?" Cruz spread his arms wide, and Javi scoffed.

"Not that big, siwwy. Our cweak is wittle. But it was pwobably this big!" He spread his arms in a miniature version of what Cruz had done. "I have to go tell Mimi!"

He raced to the house, the excitement of the moment fueling his steps.

Cruz stared after him. "He loves her."

"And she loves them." Was that hard for him to see? To hear? It had to be when he'd grown up feeling like a second-class citizen in his own house. The slap of the back door echoed down the hill. Rory sighed softly. "It will be hard for them to have her gone. Rosa is all they've known for the last two years. They've already experienced a lot of sadness and change in their little lives."

"You don't think I should take them back to New York with me."

New York.

She hadn't been down to the city in several years. While she'd loved the quick-paced energy of Manhattan, she'd never thought of it in terms of raising a family. And yet millions of people did it. "Cruz, these two will bloom and grow wherever you plant them, as long as they're loved. Kids are resilient, and Lily and Javi have never had a father figure. You'll be good for them. And I expect they'll be good for you, too." She believed that wholeheartedly. The only problem was, if he was going back to the city with the kids, what was she doing kissing him in the vineyard?

She didn't kiss casually, so when he started to turn her way, she backed up a few steps. "There's shade in the front of the house, and that's the best way to paint, midsummer. I'm going to get started."

He studied her for a moment, then nodded. "And I'll get back to work down here. The busier I am, the easier all of this is."

He moved down the next row, maneuvering the thick wire with a twist of his hand in a movement that seemed natural and synchronized.

He fit here.

She saw it. He didn't. Maybe the old emotions made being here too much of a hardship. He'd told her that people with money weren't overcomers.

He was wrong. A kid who grew up feeling unloved had a great deal to overcome. Money might make some choices easier, but it didn't pave the way to happiness.

Her father had unloaded the paint cans onto the shaded porch. He'd set up a ladder, too. She grabbed a scraper, climbed up and began to fix years of neglect, one board at a time. How she wished a sorrowful heart could be mended as easily.

Chapter Eleven

Cruz started work in the vineyard the next morning, thinking of Rory.

He'd kissed her. He'd kissed Rory Gallagher right here in the sun-drenched vines. He'd taken her into his arms and kissed her, and he'd do it again, given the chance.

But how could it work between them?

She was right to step away even though he was pretty sure she'd enjoyed that kiss as much as he had. She'd melted into his arms, into his embrace.

But within a few weeks he'd be sending an updated résumé to a Manhattan recruiter. Then he'd meet suit after suit while eating overpriced food during interviews at upscale restaurants where no one in their right mind would call him sweet thing or darlin'. And he'd be looking for a bigger apartment downstate, one big enough for two small children.

Air-conditioning and high-speed internet. Your very words. And with hedge funds in decline, why not branch out? Chart your own path? Why does it have to be New York City?

"Cruz?" Regina interrupted his thoughts. "Your mother's awake."

"Good." He stowed the thought temporarily as he made his way into his mother's room. "Hey, Mom."

Her eyes blinked open when she heard his voice. She held out a hand. He drew up a stool next to her bed and took her hand in his. "How are we doing?"

"I am tired, Cruz."

He saw the truth in that and nodded.

She breathed softly, then redirected her gaze outside. "I see you working there. I saw the arm and the scythe working, so much like your father. His ways, his style, his urge to get it done the right way."

"I may have inherited that trait from both of you." He pressed her hand lightly. "It's not a bad characteristic."

"It isn't, but I made it too important, Cruz." Now she brought her eyes back to his. "I made money and work and status too important and it ruined things."

"With Dad."

"And with my son, because I didn't take the time to be a good mother. How foolish, Crusberto." She peered at him as if her vision was being tested. "I should not have been careless in my love for you, so when Elina brought the children to me, I had a second chance. A second chance to fix what I messed up the first time. Never did I think she'd leave and not return, or I'd have fixed things, legally. And then it was too late."

He leaned in and asked the question he hated having to ask. "Why did she go back? Why would she leave her children here and go back to a place where danger awaited her at every turn? If you escape once and return, the cartels will make sure you never have the chance to escape again. Why would she risk that? Was money so important? Why couldn't you give her a job here? That would have solved so many problems, Mother." He didn't add that she'd most likely be alive. He was pretty sure Rosa understood that.

She bit her lower lip, watching the breeze flutter the vining branches leading down the hill. "There was a third child, Crusberto."

The pain of that admission darkened her features.

"Maria. She was the oldest, and they kept her separate from Elina because what mother would leave her child? She was the anchor meant to weigh your cousin down, but when she realized the hopelessness, she escaped with Lily and Javi, with him just a baby at the time. But she couldn't find peace here, knowing she'd left her child."

A third child. One he knew nothing about. "She went back for Maria."

"She looked at me and said, 'Aunt Rosa, how can a mother forget her child? God has given me you, and I know you will keep these two safe, but how can I embrace the freedom of this great country, knowing my child is held captive? I can't. I must go and try to bring her out. Bring her to safety. To freedom.'"

"So she still might be down there, trying to free Maria?"

Tears slipped down his mother's cheeks. "No. I hoped and prayed, then a note came from a cousin last year. It said many were killed for disobedience, as an example to others. Elina and Maria were part of that group."

The news sat like a brick in his chest. He wished he could have made a difference. "Why didn't she come to me? I had the means to help. Money can sometimes open even the worst of doors."

Rosa shook her head. "She was embarrassed by her choices. You had done so well, studied so hard. She said you were like a shining star, always listening to what I said, trying your best. She loved your success but didn't want you to see what she'd become. You told her not to go, remember?" She turned fading eyes his way. "You said you'd help her with college, that you'd work to help pay her way, and that you could go together."

He'd forgotten that old promise, the words of a young man beginning a whole new adventure. "I think I wanted her there more for me than for her."

"You loved each other. You were *famiglia*. I learned too late to treasure that bond, my son." She squeezed his hand lightly. "I don't want that same lost time for you, or for the children. I know I am not deserving of your forgiveness."

Did forgiveness have to be deserved? Or should it just be freely given, the way Steve suggested?

"But if you can look after these children as your own, as part of your family, then I can die in peace."

Her hand felt cool in his.

He didn't want her skin to chill. He wanted it to be warm and vibrant and tanned like it always had been this time of year. He wanted the second chance people talked about. He gripped her hand more firmly, sharing his warmth. "Or you could stay alive and boss us around a while more."

She almost smiled. Because he wanted her around? Or because he'd teased her?

Her eyes drifted shut. He stared, watching for

breath, and when she breathed the normal rhythm of sleep, his heart began beating again.

"She went back to sleep?" Regina slipped into the room on quiet-soled shoes. "Her heart is frail and her body is tired, but coming home has been good for her, Cruz. It was a noble thing to do. You're a good son to think of it."

Noble and *good*.

Two words that hadn't been applied to Cruz for a long time. Simple words that felt right.

He leaned down, kissed his mother's cheek and walked into the kitchen. He started to call Chen when a commotion drew his attention outside.

He crossed the broad foyer of the event center, opened the door and stood perfectly still, watching.

A large truck had pulled into the nearest parking lot. Three men were carrying pieces of scaffolding to the shaded western side of the house, while two other men worked to fasten the pieces together.

Two women were directing a crew of teenagers on weeding the front gardens.

Badge and Jim Reilly walked his way. "Pete said your irrigation system was down, and I figured Jim and I could have a look at it. That's what I did best, back in the day. If something broke, I fixed it."

"I'll show them where it is," offered Pete as he jogged their way. "I got held up in town. They brought little Dave home and I had to swing by and take a quick peek. Who would have thought a baby would give you such a good lease on life?"

"Ain't a thing like it," agreed Jim.

Another truck pulled in, marked Grace Haven Diner on the side, and when it pulled up in the shade just south of the porch, Sadie hopped out one side while Gus Koulos jumped out of the other. She waved to Cruz and he walked toward her while Pete took Badge and Jim to the vineyard pumping station.

"We heard there was most likely goin' to be hungry people about, so we figured we'd fire up the portable grill today. Feed a few folks some old-fashioned pancakes for breakfast and burgers for lunch. With Mama Rula's potato salad, of course," Sadie added. "I promised Rory we'd have that on hand, and Mama stayed up late last night, makin' it herself."

"Who's running the diner?" Cruz asked.

"Two of the day girls and Sal's in the kitchen, same as usual. Although from the sounds of things, most of the mornin' regulars will be right here, workin'." She waved to the gardening crew, and as she did, two more cars pulled in filled with people. Some had rakes and hoes. Others had trowels and baskets. Older women wore big floppy hats to shade from the sun, while the teen crews were decked out in tanks, shorts and flip-flops.

"Rory did this?"

"Most assuredly," Sadie told him as Gus set up a table for servingware. "She got the ball rollin', tellin' the boys what was needed, and when they heard, they got to yakkin' 'bout somethin' other than box scores, and here we are. Family. Friends. Free food." She gave him a broad grin as Gus hooked up a long, thick electric cable to the porch. "I'm hopin' Rosa won't be bothered by the noise."

"I think she'll be fine. I think she'll be ecstatic," he added. "How can I help?"

"You and I are in the grape, just like yesterday."

Pete came up behind him and clapped him on the back. "Kate's staying with Kimberly today, but we've got a couple of off-duty officers stopping by with some equipment to fix that clogged ditch around back. That will get rid of the weed and algae problem. And Rory's keeping the kids in town for the afternoon so they're not underfoot. We figured that was best," he added. "I hope it's all right."

All these people, scaffolding, equipment… "Yes, it's a great idea. I can't believe she did this." His mind was having a hard time with what his eyes were seeing. He was amazed by Rory's thoughtfulness, to go to the older guys and tell them what was needed.

It's not that he didn't expect her to be kind. It was just that he didn't expect anyone to be this kind *to him*.

It felt weird and wonderful at the same time.

"Taking care of one another, son." Pete swept the work crew a quiet gaze. "Best thing a town can do."

"I guess."

He worked steadily with Pete all morning. A group of teens brought tall plastic cups of iced tea and lemonade around to all the workers.

Five Mennonite ladies came midday and set up a dessert table of cookies, cakes and pies, the kind of pie he'd missed for so long. And at the end of the day, two and a half sides of the house were scraped and painted, the front gardens were weeded and mulched, and the grass was mowed, the edges trimmed.

And perfectly trimmed grapevines marched row on row, down to the creek for over half of the vineyard, a job well done.

A long, sleek car pulled up late in the afternoon. A woman climbed out, surveyed the property and came his way as he was thanking the Grace Haven Community Church Women's Group for their help. "You're Cruz Maldonado, aren't you?"

"Yes." He reached out to shake her hand, then realized how stained and dirty his were, and shrugged. "Sorry. And you are?"

"Melanie Carson of Carson & Carson Realty. This is gorgeous," she went on, as the ladies finished trimming out a long-neglected rose bed. "I forgot what a stunning piece of property this is."

"It's been a wonderful day, for sure."

She handed him a professional card. "Cruz, I'm not sure what your plans are, but my brother and I have the top real estate team in the area. We do both commercial and residential. If you decide to sell at any time, call us. We'd be happy to represent you and this beautiful property."

"You selling, Cruz?" One of the older women peered up at him. "Can't blame you if you do, it's not easy keepin' up a place like this."

"And it's not exactly a quick trip from New York," added another. "Though I've never been a big-city woman myself."

"I'm not sure what my plans will be, but I can't thank you ladies enough for the gift of your time." It felt awkward to have a Realtor here, talking about selling when all these nice people were generously donating their time.

"You can't beat the church ladies for knowing how to trim a yard." Melanie Carson nodded their way. "If anyone can get a place in shape, it's this crew. They're renowned."

Her compliment drew their smiles, but when she

very carefully avoided the dirt and weed pile on her way back to her car, a couple of the ladies exchanged looks and Cruz was pretty sure Melanie Carson wasn't one to get her hands dirty.

"Cruz?" Regina called his name from the front door. She'd helped his mother into the rented wheelchair, and guided her out onto the porch. "Rosa wanted to see what was going on."

He hurried her way. Would she be upset? Overwhelmed?

Regina steered the chair toward the ramp, then guided it down.

"Rosa!" The garden women called her name, waved and smiled, and the look on his mother's face, seeing her gardens in order once more... Cruz would remember that look forever.

Regina pushed her farther, then turned the chair. "What do you think?"

Rosa put a hand to her heart, but not in pain. In joy. "It looks as it did before. When Hector and I were both here, working together. The vineyard..." She sighed, smiling as she spotted the neat rows beyond the big house. "Oh, Cruz, your father would be so proud. It looks just like when he was here. You remembered!"

He leaned down, glad for the happiness this brought her. "You never forget how to capture the grape, Mom."

Her smile grew deeper. "His words from his son. As it should be."

She started coughing then. The cough shook her, and when Regina began to steer her back into the house, Rosa lifted a hand. "A minute longer, all right? A minute more to see. Just to see. And remember."

Her gaze swept the house, the yard, the gardens, the

walkways, the vineyard and she sighed, happy. "We can go in now." She whispered the words to Regina, then yawned. "But I am so glad to have seen this. All of this. Thank you."

Her voice was soft, but it seemed like most people heard her. Folks waved. They wished her well, and a couple came over to give her gentle hugs.

And as Regina backed the wheelchair through the front door, Cruz caught his mother's eye.

She smiled at him. Just him. As if he mattered more than he'd ever thought possible.

"We've got to head out, Cruz." The painters had put away their supplies. "But we'll be back first thing tomorrow to finish up."

It felt odd, not paying them. Downright weird. But when they clapped him on the back and moved to their cars, he knew they didn't expect pay. His gratitude was enough.

By the time everyone had left, his mother had fallen asleep, the evening aide had relieved Regina and he needed to see Rory and the kids.

How could he thank her?

How could he make her understand what her self-lessness meant? He wasn't sure, but as he climbed into his car, he intended to figure it out.

Chapter Twelve

"Of course I couldn't believe the whole kit and caboodle sold, so I called my brother straightaway." Flora Belker set her hands on her hips as Lily and Javi played with her small dog in her neatly trimmed yard. "He said the whole lot was gone, plus all the buildings, sold to an Asian person lickety-split, as if there was no time to wait. I'm so sorry, Rory. I was hoping we could take that back corner and sell it to you. I know we'd all like to see your school plans take hold."

Blocked again.

Was her plan just a pipe dream? Was she walking the wrong road? Was there a reason it kept getting put off? Or were these simply normal circumstances and she needed to persevere?

Disappointment mushroomed inside her. How could anything happen if she couldn't find a place to house the school? Zoning in Grace Haven was guarded zealously by the town board and the zoning commission. Their goal of keeping the town's old-time charm while still supporting small businesses was like walking a tightrope. Asking them to change the zoning on a residential building wasn't going to work, but with few sites available, her goal of a January opening didn't look good.

But she needed to soothe Flora's feelings, because the older woman appeared quite distraught. "Miss Flora, you know how these things go. Whenever God shuts a door, He opens a window. This will all work out in His timing. I know it."

"Do you think so?" Flora hugged Rory's arm as the children petted the tricolor dog. "I told Thelma we should have gone with Carson Realty because they're more hometown, but she proved me wrong with this quick sale, then Melanie Carson herself stopped by Casa Blanca while we were cleaning out the roses, and let me tell you, she wasted no time handing Cruz her card and letting him know they'd love to sell the place for him."

Another emotional blow hit Rory. "So he's selling?"

Flora raised her hands. "He didn't say he was and didn't say he wasn't, but what would keep him here? A successful businessman like him, with all he's got to offer the world? And the upkeep on a place like that is ridiculous, I tell you. But then I'm old and maybe it's not such a burden on the young. Pookie, play nice," she scolded the shaggy dog when Javi raced across her thick green grass, the dog leaping and nipping at his heels.

"Javi." The little guy ran to Rory's side, overwrought. He was wild. The dog was wild. Time to go home where she could digest all of this. "Come on, Miss Lily. We've got to go."

"Okay." Calmer than her busy brother, she waved to

the little dog and moved toward Rory. "Are we going to see Mimi today?"

She'd kept them in town on purpose, to avoid danger with the various work crews and cars moving in and out of the Casa Blanca parking lot. Things would probably have calmed down by now. "I'll text my dad and see how things are going, okay? Let's have a quick supper first, then we'll drive over if she's awake."

"Can we have peanut butter and jelly again? I love it when you make that, Miss Rory."

Happy with simple things. But how would they handle Manhattan?

Not your kids. Not your concern.

She pushed herself to remember that all the way home. They ate their sandwiches in the shade of the thick maple tree, then she walked them to the lakeshore. They dashed into the sand, each holding a bucket filled with sand shovels and plastic cups.

Priceless moments. Kids being kids.

She was reminding herself that kids did well in all kinds of circumstances when Cruz slipped onto the grassy knoll beside her a few minutes later. Her pulse went up, but the common sense of her brain jumped in to squelch the quick beat of her heart.

"How'd it go today?"

"You." He cradled her face between his two beautiful hands, surprised her with a sweet but quick kiss, then held her gaze. "I can't believe you arranged for all that to happen. I still can't believe it *did* happen, and how much better everything looks. It's amazing. *You're* amazing. Thank you, Rory."

She might have been able to resist his thanks. His words. Or his kiss. But the combination made her long for more of the same. But what was the point? She waved off his thanks with as much nonchalance as she could muster. "I just put the word out. The good hearts of Grace Haven did the rest. Are they coming back tomorrow to finish?"

"Yes." He looked so relaxed, so pleased, and quite different from the man who'd rolled into town with a monster-sized chip on his shoulder. "You should have seen the look on my mother's face. She was positively radiant when she saw the front of the house looking like it used to. I don't know how to thank you for that look of joy you gave her. Words aren't nearly enough."

They would be if they were the right words, but there was a reason love-at-first-sight romance only happened in stories. Fiction had its place and she was pretty sure Grace Haven was rooted in good old reality most days. "Words are plenty. I'm glad you're pleased, Cruz. I'm glad you two have had time to just be mother and son, even if it's only a short while. Nothing can erase memories like these."

"You're right." He braced himself on his hands and sat back. "My memories of Grace Haven weren't the kind of thing I dug up on a regular basis before."

"And now?"

"It's funny." He gazed out at the lake, the kids, the soft wind shifting thin willow branches this way and that. "I'm remembering a bunch of things that weren't so bad and I wonder if the bad stuff sticks better and messes up how we see things as kids."

Her anguish over Millicent's choices proved him right. "I think it does. Kids don't have the maturity to discern, so hurt gets magnified." She hesitated, then went on. "I've been wanting to start my preschool for the past few years as a payback for something that went bad in high school. I'd promised God I'd do something to make up for my selfishness back then. Creating this school is my personal pay-it-forward. It doesn't fix the old wrongs, but if it's a help to others, that can't be a bad thing."

"I can't imagine you being selfish, Rory."

She made a face of doubt. "Well, I was a kid and kids do stupid things. Anyway, I planned and plotted and then Dad got sick. When his treatment took a year in Texas, that meant Mom would be gone. We all jumped on board, no questions asked, because that was the right thing to do. And when they wanted to retire, I knew I might be needed to help at Kate & Company, and that was fine because families should help one another. But this summer I've come so close." She set her hands on her pulled-up knees and leaned forward, watching the kids build castles in the sand. "My paperwork is finally done, I've got everything lined up, except once again there is no available commercial space to rent or buy. The site I loved, the one I talked to Miss Flora about, managed to sell in a nanosecond. She felt bad, but it wasn't her fault." She shrugged. "It wasn't anyone's fault, it's just how things go. So is God putting hurdles in my path because it isn't the way I'm supposed to go? Or are these normal circumstances I need to face and overcome?" She frowned, still gazing out. "I have no idea, but I've either got to find a way to make the school work or get a full-time teaching position. I can't tread water forever. Right?"

He had to tell her.

There was no choice, not really, because when the

Washburn deal became public knowledge, so would his identity. Better she hear it now from him than be surprised down the road.

Gentle waves lapped against the shore, lazy rolls of water against sun-bleached sand. And on that sand, two children played, kids who had been brought to freedom against strong odds. As a woman who respected faith and truth, she deserved that from him. "Rory."

"Hmm?" She looked back at him, brows lifted.

She was so beautiful. So wise, so sweet, so innocent in her own way, an innocence that was strengthened by faithful resolve. He held her gaze, knowing that what he was about to say would upset her, but he had no choice. "I bought the Belker complex."

Confusion shifted her brows together. "I don't understand."

"I saw that it was going up for sale when I first got here and knew real estate here was prime. I had my associate put in an offer immediately. It was a generous offer, and the family agreed quickly."

"Then *you* own the house." Excitement cleared the confusion from her face. "You own the house I want to buy. Can I put in an offer on the Belker homestead, overlooking Jackson Road? How perfect would that be?"

"Rory." He swallowed hard, then put his hands on her shoulders, wishing he didn't have to confess the rest. "I resold it about thirty-six hours later."

"You what?" She looked stunned.

"My associate cut a deal with Washburn Hotels. They'd been looking in the area, but everything sells quickly, and they could never find the right location. I knew there was a shortage of hotel rooms when I came to town, and it just made sense because it takes forever to get commercial zoning approval here."

She pinned him with a cool gaze of assessment. "You sold it at a profit, of course."

"Of course." He held her gaze, got the gist and shook his head. "I didn't know you wanted it until after it was sold. If I'd known, Rory—"

"If you'd known, what would you have done, Cruz?" She stood, dusted off the seat of her pants and called the kids to pack up their things, then turned back to him.

He stood, too. "Rory, there have to be other places around. I'll help you find one. I'll—"

"Stop." She looked him square in the eye. This wasn't the compassionate kindergarten-teacher side of her. This was warrior Rory, like he'd seen the morning of Lily's dream. "I get it, Cruz. Money first. I saw it before, and you told me, but I chose to believe what I wanted to believe. Not what was in front of my eyes."

"That's not true. I didn't know you wanted it until after I made the deal. How was I supposed to know that you had plans for that one building?"

She didn't flinch, didn't waver. "It's got nothing to do with knowing or not knowing, don't you see? It's a simple case of doing what you do best—making money. You saw the chance to turn a quick profit…"

That was exactly what he'd done, so he couldn't fault her reasoning.

"…and didn't think there was anyone else around who might have a want or a need. And because you have quick cash at your disposal…"

Again, true.

"...you're able to cut deals at lightning speed, while the common folk follow the rules, going step by step."

"Rory, I—" He started to protest, but she raised up a hand, a very casual but firm hand.

"I trusted you, Cruz. How silly you must think I am, walking around town, talking about a school for needy kids, so absolutely naive. Well, I should thank you."

She didn't look like she wanted to thank him. She looked like she wanted to sock him in the jaw.

"I'm less naive now than I was thirty minutes ago, that's for sure. And now—" she laid a soft, ivory hand on Lily's dark hair "—I'm going to take our little friends home for a quick shower and bed. Tomorrow is their last day of school and we've got a fun day planned, so we can't be up late tonight. Say good-night to Cruz, guys."

"Do we have to?" Javi lifted puppy-dog eyes her way. "I was just gonna see if Cwuz would take us to see Mimi." He tipped a big bright smile of entreaty Cruz's way. "For just a wittle while? Pwease?"

"We'll go home when you say." Lily grabbed hold of Cruz's hand on one side, Rory's on the other, and for a moment they looked like a Norman Rockwell scene, the kids begging Mom and Dad for extra time at the beach. "We won't make Mimi too tired, okay?"

But they weren't Mom and Dad, and he'd just dashed her plans. Was it his fault she lived in a hot real estate market?

No.

But he should have told her the week before, before she'd had time to get her hopes up.

"She's sleeping, guys," Cruz began. "I'll bring you to see her tomorrow, okay? When she's awake."

Javi looked disappointed. So did Lily, but then she

threw her arms around Cruz and hugged him. "Then we'll see you and Mimi tomorrow, okay? It's a deal!"

"Will you tell Mimi I wuv her?" Javi tipped his gaze up, eyes wide. "Like this much!" He stretched his arms wider than he had for the fish, pointing tiny fingers as far and straight as he could. "I'll see her tomorrow, too! After school, okay?"

What could he say? "After school. I'll come get you."

Rory took one of their hands in each of hers and started walking away.

He wanted to stop her, make her listen and see his side. Would she glance back, over her shoulder?

She didn't. She paused at the road, waiting until it was safe to cross, then escorted the children away from the water, the beach, the breeze and him.

Was it wrong to have made the purchase like he had?

Not in Manhattan circles.

But things were different here.

Though one look at the bustling Main Street seemed to say otherwise. A large segment of people in Grace Haven worked hard to make a good living in their busy, quaint town, and if they saw a way to make money, they did it. Otherwise the real estate market wouldn't be so tight.

It wasn't *business* that was different, he realized. It was the heart of a woman with a dream, a dream he'd messed up with his quick action.

A text from Chen buzzed in as Rory and the kids disappeared from sight.

Rodney froze accounts.

A power play, typical of his former boss. Rodney liked to toy with people in a game of cat and mouse. Was Chen smart enough to have kept his personal accounts away from the business?

Business, right? Not both?

A few seconds later, a text came back and it wasn't the answer he wanted to hear.

Both. My records were tied into my stock options.

He didn't tell his colleague that was a dumb move. He was pretty sure Chen realized that. And at the moment, he had a dying mother and two kids to look out for, and he'd probably just ruined his best chance at the kind of relationship he'd never thought possible.

Maybe it would have been possible if he hadn't been so stuck on himself…and money.

He called Chen. The call went straight to voice mail. Either Chen had turned his phone off or wasn't ready to talk to the man who'd cost him his lucrative position in the financial district.

An hour ago he'd been delighted with the progress on the house and the joy that gave his mother. Rory's reaction put a damper on that.

She'd instigated a town-wide effort to help him because she cared about others, so maybe that was the chasm between them. She put others first, all the time.

Cruz hadn't done that since he was a boy.

Could he relearn? Could he turn off the high-finance mind-set he'd been using for years?

He pulled into the parking area and stepped out of

his car. Upscale car, trimmed-out, mansion-style event center, gorgeous yard, beautiful gardens…

Standing there, surrounded by the beauty of where he'd been raised, he knew he fit here, too. Maybe too well. He checked in on Rosa. The evening nurse was quietly doing crossword puzzles as his mother slept nearby. He explained he'd be next door, then got back in the car, drove to the abbey and knocked on Steve Gallagher's door.

Steve came around the corner of the sprawling stone complex. "Cruz, what's up? Is it Rosa?"

"No." He made a face of contrition. "It's me."

Steve studied him. "I'm weeding in the back. The crew at your house inspired me and it's cool enough to tackle now. Come talk while I work."

Steve walked through the gate of a fenced-in vegetable garden and picked up a hoe. He started working his way down a row of not-so-tall corn. "What's going on?"

Cruz looked over the big garden and Steve. "Got another hoe?"

"To your left. Tara was helping me earlier."

He found the hoe and began clearing the next row. "I've messed up, Steve."

A tiny muscle in Steve's cheek shifted up. "Welcome to life. Are we talking current, past or both?"

"Both."

"Fix it."

"It's not that easy," he began, but Steve turned, rested his arms on the hoe and frowned.

"Nobody said anything about easy. But everything is fixable, Cruz. Two weeks ago, would you have expected to be here, staying at Casa Blanca, helping your mother?"

That question required no thought. "No."

"And yet…" Steve looked from Cruz to the vineyard stretching between the properties.

"Yet here I am."

"Yup." Steve went back to hoeing, stroke by stroke. "Of course your life is in New York."

Was it? It *had* been, he realized, as the hoe blade nipped noxious quack grass out of the ground.

"And your job is there."

"Not anymore. The boss got upset that I was staying to help Mom and let me go. And fired my team. So my choices affected a lot of innocent people."

Steve faced him now, eyes wide. "He fired your group because you wanted to spend time with your dying mother?"

The shock on Steve's face underscored Rodney's depravity. "Yes."

"Why would you consider staying in a place like that?" Steve didn't wait for him to answer—he waved a preacher-style hand around, indicating the broad, open fields, the majesty of the woods, the lake, the surrounding patchwork-quilt countryside. "When God provides this?"

"You mean why would I stay at Randolph & Gordon? Or in New York?"

"Either."

He stared at Steve, pondering the question.

Why *was* he planning to go back? What was in the city that he couldn't have here in Grace Haven?

All I need is air-conditioning and high-speed internet.

He'd summed it up when he first came to town. As long as he had a flat surface and high-speed internet, he had an office.

So why not here?

"I mean, if you need to go back, then you do what you have to do, but a smart man like you, a man who's already made a lot of money..." Steve kept hoeing as he spoke, so Cruz did, too. "Why not shift your office here? It's not like you've got inventory to move. It's you and a computer, right? And good phone service. All of which we've got."

And the kids would love to stay in the Finger Lakes, to grow up in the only place they'd known peace, love and joy. "I could do that. There's risk involved, of course, but my clients trust me."

"And if you look around here, there's still a fair share of old money looking for investments, and new money looking to avoid taxation," Steve pointed out. "A lot of folks here could use your expertise. It might not be the huge bankroll folks take for granted in the city, but who needs that kind of money?"

He didn't, Cruz realized. He'd wanted to make it big to show his mother he *could* make it big, but then the urge for more had grabbed hold and never let go. Somewhere along the way big ceased being enough because there was always something bigger and better, just out of reach.

"It gets to be like a cancer." Steve leaned on his hoe once more. "Wanting more, never thinking it's enough. Blessed are the meek, for they shall inherit the earth."

"I've never been accused of being meek," Cruz admitted.

"Neither had your mother, but when she saw the grief her choices brought—losing her husband's love, losing her son's respect—she grabbed at the chance to make a difference to Lily and Javi. She changed her heart and her mind," Steve reminded him. "If your mother can manage to do that at her age, then you've got no excuse, son. We make the first step to humility by putting others first."

Chen. His family. Rory.

It came clear, right then, as if the sun shone brighter and the shadows grew shorter. "What if I mess up?"

"Nobody learns to play ball or build a business by getting it all right the first time. We practice. And when we fall down—"

"We pick ourselves up."

"There you go." They'd finished the two long rows of corn, and when Steve slapped his neck, he set the hoe aside. "Mosquitoes. I'm calling it a day."

"Thank you, sir." Cruz set his hoe against the fence and followed Steve out the gate. "I appreciate it."

"Nothing like solving the world's problems over God's own dirt." Steve stuck out his hand and shook Cruz's. "I'm here whenever you need me, Cruz."

"Like old times."

Steve smiled. "Exactly."

Putting others first.

He resolved to put that into practice, first thing in the morning. Once Chen was calm enough to talk, he'd invite him on board. He'd make a plan and work his plan, the same way he'd charted success all along, with one major difference.

This time the plan would have others' goals and needs in the front seat. He got back to Casa Blanca, and pulled into the drive. His phone jangled at the same moment the front door opened. The evening nurse came through the door as Regina's car pulled in behind his.

"She's fading." The nurse glanced at the phone in his hand. "I tried your number but it went to voice mail, so I called Regina."

Regina started for the door. "Let's check this out."

Cruz hurried inside. He crossed to the hospital bed, not thinking of washing his hands or cleaning up, only thinking of one thing: his mother. "Mom?"

He bent low. Regina turned the lights up slightly. She moved in from the other side of the bed. She pressed two fingers to the inside of Rosa's wrist and checked her breathing, then stepped back. "We're slowing down, Cruz."

His heart stuttered. His throat went tight. "Are you sure? Isn't there anything we can do? The kids wanted to see her, they—"

He couldn't say anymore, thinking of how Lily and Javi had grabbed hold of him a little while ago, sending messages of love to Mimi.

Put others first.

He leaned down, holding Rosa's hand. "Mom? Javi and Lily want you to know they love you. They love you so much. And they're so glad you took care of them, and kept them here and gave them such a good home. They love you, Mom." He didn't think his throat could grow thicker, but it did. He leaned closer yet. "I love you, Mom."

Cool fingers squeezed his hand. Her eyes fluttered open, just long enough to see him. To smile at him. Her head shook as she tried to speak, the struggle for words a harsh hurdle. "You don't have to say anything," he told her. He leaned in and kissed her cool, pale forehead. "I know you loved me. Give Dad a hug for me, okay?"

Her eyes went wide, then relaxed. Her chin dipped down as if nodding, and then she whispered, "Yes."

One word, one tiny, soft-spoken word, and then she eased back against the raised pillow. Her eyes closed. Her breathing paused.

And she was gone.

Rory read the text just before ten that night. She walked outside, past the trees, past the town lights and read it again, under the thick blanket of stars.

Mom has passed away. I'll be over in the morning to tell the children. Steve is helping with details.

She was glad he had Steve close by. She was glad he'd had time to make amends with his mother. But she would miss her cantankerous old friend. And with Rosa gone, Cruz would have no reason not to sell out quickly, pack the kids' bags and head back to New York.

Rosa's death would impact the children in a myriad of ways. They would miss the only grandmother figure they'd ever known. They would miss the countryside they laughed and played in. But the court order insisting on supervised visits with the children would be removed, and then what? Did Javi and Lily go to Cruz by default?

She could only hope and pray that was the choice. Cruz loved them. It was clear in every interaction. He'd figure out the little stuff in time, the ins and outs of raising kids, but he had the means and the love and he was family. Surely the court wouldn't insist on anything else. Would it?

She couldn't sleep. Was he faring any better?

Probably not.

By the time the children got up in the morning, the last thing she wanted to do was put on a happy face for the final day of summer pre-K, but she did it. And when Cruz arrived just after eight o'clock, her mother let him in with a hug.

"Hey." He sat on the bench along the back of the table. The kids faced him, bright-eyed and excited, but when Lily looked at him, her bright smile faded.

"Is our Mimi gone?" The words came out low. She held Cruz's gaze. Her chin quivered. His throat convulsed, and Rory slipped down to the floor next to Lily and grasped her hand. "She's gone home to heaven to be with God. With your mama, too."

"Like your dad?" Lily aimed the question to Cruz, but held tight to Rory's hand.

He nodded. "She's with my dad now. They're all together."

"But we can still go see her after school, right?"

Javi glanced from one to the other, confused. "'Cause you pwomised us."

"We can't, darling." Rory pressed a kiss to his cheek.

"But you *pwomised*." Javi slipped off his seat and threw a scrap of toast onto the table. "Last night we wanted to see our Mimi and you pwomised we'd see her today. I heard you!"

Rory wished she could take back their casually spoken words from the night before, but it was too late.

Javi raced through the screen door, into the yard. He kicked the picnic table again and again, a sad, angry little fellow, not knowing what just happened to turn his life upside down again.

"I'll go." Cruz stood up. He leaned down and kissed Lily's cheek. "We'll be okay, honey. I promise."

She didn't look up at him. She didn't look anywhere. Eyes down, she stared at the kitchen table, a little girl who'd heard lots of promises, Rory expected, and many that were broken.

Cruz walked outside quietly.

Rory took the seat next to Lily. "I'm sorry, darling."

Lily sighed, then shrugged as if this was same old, same old. Her family had been shattered apart through violence and death multiple times. "I'll call Glenda and have her take the morning class, and I'll stay here with you."

Lily shook her head. She got out of the chair and raised her gaze, her jaw firm. "I want to go to pre-K with you. It's our special day. I don't want to miss our special day, Miss Rory." Solemn and sober, she faced Rory with gumption far beyond her chronological years.

"But—"

Kate peeked around the doorway from the living room. She waved to Rory, and when Rory looked her way, she made a slicing motion across her neck to indicate she should cut the conversation.

Since she had precious little experience with small children and death, she took her mother's advice. "Then that's what we'll do, honey. Let's get our stuff together."

She walked out of the house with Lily a few minutes later. Javi raced her way, ignoring Cruz. He grabbed her hand and clung tight. "Are we g-g-going to school now?"

She nodded, but gave him one last chance. "Unless you'd rather stay with Cruz this morning? I'm sure he'd love to have your company."

"No." Javi didn't look at Cruz. He looked up at her and held on tight to her hand. "No, I just want to be wif you, Miss Wory."

Her heart ached. Her throat went tight, because she loved these two children and they'd just suffered another grievous loss in the midst of chaos. They'd be gone soon, and Cruz would be gone soon, and maybe that was their destiny. If so, she'd wish nothing but the best for them. But for the moment, this one last day of school, she was willing to keep their morning as normal as possible. "Then we'll see Cruz after our celebration, okay?"

Javi didn't look convinced that he wanted to see Cruz. Was he angry at him for Rosa's death? Or just mad that he would never have a chance to see her?

"Okay." Lily clung tight, whispered the word and didn't look up.

Rory did.

Sorrow deepened Cruz's gaze. He looked down at the kids, and didn't try to push them to change their minds. He just nodded and said, "I'll pick you up after school."

The two kids exchanged looks and trudged forward, eyes down, and it was a somber trio taking the stroll up to the White Church one last time.

Chapter Thirteen

Rory hadn't thought her heart could ache this much, but it did.

It hadn't rained in weeks prior to Rosa's passing, but it didn't just rain the day of her funeral. It poured.

A large tent was erected in the hillside cemetery, but wind-whipped rain darkened an already somber occasion.

The next morning Judge Murdoch awarded Cruz custody of the children. It was the right thing to do, but Rory had grown accustomed to their funny flip-flopped sleeping schedules, the earnest chatter and the joyful squeals of innocence. But right now, with Rosa gone and their future unsure, there hadn't been many happy outbursts. The brother-and-sister duo would play, smile, then remember…and the looks of joy would fade.

She'd overseen their packing, and she'd made sure Gator was tucked into Javi's bag. She'd packed their favorite books, a list of best-loved foods and the jar of Fluff for peanut-butter and Fluff sandwiches, a new culinary delight. Then she'd kissed them soundly and had her father drive them up to Casa Blanca.

If she drove them, she'd cry.

If Cruz came here, she'd cry.

She hated crying in front of people, so why torture herself? This way she could wipe her tears in peace, and if she went through two full boxes of tissues in three days, well, then she'd thank God she had two full boxes.

She'd submitted her grant application, having cited two possible locations she probably couldn't afford, and she'd sent out her résumé to three area elementary schools. Few positions popped open in August, but every once in a while one did, and she intended to be ready if called for an interview. After all, she scolded herself for probably the fifth time that day, she had so much to be grateful for.

Her father was in remission and back home. Her mother was on hand to help at Kate & Company, which left Rory with free time on her hands, something that hadn't happened in the past two years. And little Dave was just about the cutest thing she'd ever seen. She busied herself with him as much as she could, and refused to think of Javi and Lily, moving off to New York; of Casa Blanca, empty and fading once again; or of Cruz, finding himself at home in the crazy, frenetic chaos of Manhattan. Just because it wasn't her thing didn't make it less wonderful for the kids.

She knew that.

She just couldn't make herself believe it.

"Rory." Corinne crossed the yard with her son, Callan, later that week. "Tee is over at Emily's helping with the twins, and Callan told Dad he'd help him at Rosa's, but I've got a conference call at seven from the hospital. Would you mind running him up to Casa Blanca?"

"Casa Blanca?" Her heart leaped like a grass frog on a May afternoon. "What's Dad doing up there?"

"I guess Cruz needed a couple of last-minute things done on the farm, and Callan offered to help for his eighth-grade service project."

Rory laid an arm around her nephew's shoulders. "That's awesome, dude."

Color bit his cheeks. His sister, Tee Tee, was a chip off the old block, happy to be the center of attention like Rory's brother, Dave, had been. Callan was more like Corinne, laid-back and focused. "Shall we go right now?" she asked.

He nodded. "I promised Grandpa I'd come right after baseball practice."

"Hop in."

I will be calm, cool and collected. I will be calm, cool and collected. I will be…

Rory made herself stop reciting the line. First, it was silly. Second, it wouldn't do her a bit of good, so she'd pull up, drop Callan off and head back to town.

Her perfect plan went awry.

The first driveway had been blocked off and re-sealed. She drove to the next entrance on the far side of the house. Two moving vans sat there, back doors shut and locked, reminders of Cruz and the kids' imminent departure.

She sucked in a breath and rounded the lot, then paused near the sidewalk. "Here you go."

"Thanks, Aunt Rory!" Callan jumped out of the car, spotted Pete across the way and called out.

Pete turned.

Just as he did, Cruz moved into view, and turned Callan's way.

Oh, her heart…

Their eyes met.

He started to move her way.

A well-dressed woman came through the front door and pulled his attention. She put a beautifully manicured hand on his arm, and he paused to listen.

Rory took the hint and quietly swung the car in a quick arc toward the road.

She didn't look back. Why would she?

Because you're smitten, crabbed her conscience. *Because you think the world of this guy and you got your nose bent out of shape over a real estate deal. What's the matter with you? Were you looking to find fault with him? Because I think the guy's tried real hard to be a good son to his mother, to take charge of two kids and to get all of Rosa's things in order.*

You might want to cut him some slack.

Was the internal scolding correct? Did she overreact because she was disappointed or because Cruz did something wrong?

The former, she realized.

He'd done exactly what he was trained to do, and probably what plenty of other folks in town would have done if they'd had the right connections. It didn't make him bad. It made him smart.

The doves were cooing softly when she parked the car back home. Their nestlings had flown, and the silver-gray parents had settled into a calm routine. Every year they came back, and some of the family, too.

And every year the sound of their soft voices marked morning and evening.

"Am I boring?" she asked Corinne when her sister-in-law strode outside with a glass of tea.

Corinne collapsed into a lawn chair, set her tea down and peered up at Rory. "Is this a trick question? Because trick questions are not allowed after six p.m. My shift started thirteen hours ago, sweet thing, so my brain is officially fried. But in answer to your question, no. You are *not* boring."

Rory was about to breathe a sigh of relief when Corinne added, "Predictable, maybe. But never boring."

"Semantics," Rory grumbled. She sank into the chair across from Corinne.

"Was Cruz at the house?"

Rory nodded.

"Did you talk?"

She shook her head. "He had people there. And he and Dad were working." She sighed and shrugged. "Best to just move on, anyway."

Corinne sat forward and groaned, as if even that effort was too much in the evening. "What is the matter with people today?"

"Huh?"

"You. Cruz. Young people, falling in love."

"Well, I'd hardly say love," Rory argued, although her conscience contradicted her silently. "We've only known each other a few weeks."

"Why would you think that's not enough when God

puts destiny in your path? I knew I loved your brother when I was seventeen years old, and when people made jokes about young love, I ignored them. I knew he was meant for me. And he knew it, too. Why waste time?"

"It's not that easy."

"Because you made it difficult." Corinne leaned forward again. "Listen. I had the love of my life for thirteen years. They were wonderful years, with all the ups and downs of a roller coaster, and when I lost Dave I thought I'd never recover. But I did. And the kids did." She gave Rory a frank look. "I wouldn't trade those thirteen years of wonderful for anything, Rory. Life's a risk, every day. But it's also a blessing, if we're smart enough to grab those blessings and appreciate them. And now—" she downed the rest of her tea and stood "—I'm going to pick up Tee and head home. Dad's dropping Callan off and I'm beat."

She leaned down and kissed Rory's cheek. "Don't be afraid to make bold decisions, Rory. God's got your back no matter where you're living."

She waved as she pulled out of the driveway.

Life is a blessing.

Thirteen years… She'd lost Dave over a decade ago, and had raised the two kids on her own, and she still blessed the years they had together.

Rory took Corinne's glass inside. She had to clean out the preschool rooms in the White Church tomorrow and pack stuff away. Maybe then she'd go see Cruz. Visit the kids before they headed downstate.

Avoiding the goodbyes showed lack of courage, and the kids deserved more than that. They deserved her love, right up to the day they left.

* * *

Cruz stared at Rory's retreating car.

Should he drive after her? Chase her down?

He wanted to, and Cruz couldn't say he'd ever felt that way about a woman before, especially one that thought he was a money-grubbing tycoon with little regard for others' feelings. The fact that he'd been exactly that for years didn't matter. He was changing, on purpose, but would Rory believe that?

Possibly not after he'd sold her preschool house to the highest bidder.

"Rory didn't stop in to see the kids?" Pete swept his sleeve across his brow as he came up alongside Cruz. "That's not like her."

"Probably busy."

Pete looked at Cruz. Then he turned his attention to the now empty road, then back to Cruz. "Mmm-hmm. Well, she's got a big job ahead of her tomorrow morning."

"What's she doing?"

"She's got to stash all the preschool stuff she used for the summer program. I told her I'd come by with the truck to help her move everything into the carriage house like she did last year, but I should really finish getting those stalls fixed on the lower barn before our little friends get dropped off."

Cruz jumped at the opportunity. "I'll help Rory. I'm out of practice with hammers and nails, but I've helped a lot of folks move apartments in Manhattan. If the financial stuff ever gets old, I could make money as a mover."

Pete laughed. "You're on. I can't wait to see the

inside of that barn looking like it used to, and Callan likes learning to build things. He's got a knack."

"Then we're good."

Pete nodded and strode toward the lower barn, whistling. "We're good."

Chapter Fourteen

Rory stacked boxes on one side of the hallway leading to the church stairs, then plastic totes on the other. Behind all of that she set equipment and chairs. She'd need help with the six tables, but she and her father could muscle those together. She sent him a text once everything was packed and labeled.

Ready when you are, Dad.

He texted back:

Pickup truck is on the way.

Perfect. She began hauling boxes up the narrow stairs. By the time she'd brought up box number four, a big silver pickup rolled into the lot and backed up to the door.

Her dad didn't climb out of the cab.

Cruz did.

Her heart raced. Hadn't she intended to go see him once this was done? Yes, so why was her heart all tangled up just because the tall, good-looking guy showed up unexpectedly?

He headed her way and nodded toward the stack of boxes as if he was totally unaffected. "All this is going?"

Obviously he was handling their rift far better than she was. Maybe it was good for her to know that. She nodded, but waved toward the street. "Yes, but my dad's on his way."

"He sent me."

"Is he all right?"

Cruz nodded easily as he slid one box after another into the front of the truck bed. "He's fine, just tied up at the vineyard. He's got a knack with carpentry. I don't. So he's fixing some things in the barn and I said I'd help you. Got more stuff?" He asked it casually, as if being with her was no big deal while her pulse was dancing a jig.

"A lot."

"All right." He carried totes, boxes, toys, riding toys and chairs. By the time they got to the tables, the truck was full. "Let's drop this off and come back for those."

"Okay." That meant climbing into the cab of the truck, making the short drive home and spending time together unloading.

She could do this and smile naturally, just like he was doing. If she could control the crazy urge to jump into his arms and kiss him senseless.

Fortunately, she was more mature than that, but barely.

"Where's all this going?"

"The back of our carriage house," she told him. "Dad leaves the third bay for my pre-K stuff."

"Mice don't bother it?"

"We've lost some books and art supplies in the past," she admitted. "It's a garage, so the occasional mouse is a given."

"Could we store it someplace else?"

She shook her head, eyes forward. "The price of a storage unit wouldn't offset a few crayons and yarn. The garage is fine."

"All right." He drove back to the Gallagher house, backed the truck into the designated bay and dropped the tailgate. "How about if you hop up there and slide those boxes and totes back to me? I'll stack them."

It made sense, so she did it, and by the time they were done, Cruz had stacked everything into neat sections. She had to hand it to him, his organizational skills were pretty solid. Her father would have hodge-podged the boxes into a corner. She started to jump down.

Two hands at her waist stopped her. Two big, beautiful, strong hands, with a gentle but firm grip.

She ordered her pulse to slow down.

It refused, and actually sped faster when her feet touched the ground, because Cruz didn't let go. She looked up. Met his gaze.

Her heart joined in the amplified rhythm when he smiled at her.

She knew that smile. She'd been falling head over heels for that smile and the strong, funny man behind it. He held on for long, slow ticks of the clock, then dropped his hands. "Let's get those tables."

"All right."

She cleared her head of the smile and the feel of his hands at her waist. He was just trying to help in her father's place, so to make more of it than that would be foolish on her part, and she'd had enough of that.

They loaded the tables, tucked them into the garage and closed the bay.

"Done." Cruz looked at her, triumphant.

"Yes. Thank you. It's always good to have that job out of the way."

"You do this every summer? Set everything up in the church, then break it down when preschool is done?"

"Not always the church," she reminded him. "We set up in whatever building has a room they don't mind us using. The old fire hall, church basements, a rectory basement, unused meeting rooms."

"So of course you'd want a place of your own." He didn't glance across The Square at the Belker buildings, but she knew he was thinking of it.

"That's one of the reasons," she replied, as if they were just a couple of old chums talking. "I think I'm pretty effective with kids, regardless of surroundings. I make it work, and the kids don't notice. They want love and attention and someone to teach them and be nice to them. The other reason to establish my own program is to offer kids a chance they might not get the way things are now. Kids like Lily and Javi were before you came along. Kids in loving homes but with no money for schooling, who start at a disadvantage."

"It's a solid goal, Rory." He held her gaze as if he wanted to say more, then didn't. "Your dad will be needing the truck for hauling lumber. I better head back."

"Of course." She stepped back, too, polite, just like Cruz. "Thank you for helping." She indicated the stuffed garage with a glance. "I couldn't have done it alone."

"Glad to be here." He touched the tip of the old Grace Haven Eagles ball cap he was wearing, got into the truck and drove away.

And that was that.

But it wasn't. She didn't want him to drive away, and she'd promised herself she'd see the kids. She didn't even know when he was leaving, and she'd avoided the topic on purpose so she wouldn't get silly and emotional.

She went inside, restless.

"Rory?"

She turned when Kimberly called her name, surprised. "I forgot you were here."

"Shh." Kimberly put her finger to her lips. "Davy's sleeping, and despite what they said about waking him every couple of hours to eat, I'm letting him sleep. That was the first two-hour nap I've gotten in weeks."

"Here, sit down." Rory pulled out a chair. "Do you want coffee? Can you have coffee?"

"Yes to both, but I'd rather have Mom's iced tea. Nobody makes it better. Wasn't that nice of Cruz to help you?"

Rory recognized her big sister's informational-quest expression, the one where she said one thing while ferreting out another. "Very nice. Stop probing. I do believe I explained that he'd be adopting the kids and taking them to New York, end of story, so get that gleam out of your eye."

"Of course that makes sense," offered Kimberly. "He lives in Manhattan."

"It doesn't make one bit of sense," Rory argued.

"No?" Kimberly arched a brow.

"Not when the kids are so happy here. What is there about living in a midtown high-rise that works for kids? Kids that are used to running up and down hills, playing hide-and-seek in grapevines. All I can see is total culture shock."

"I see your point." Kimberly paused, playing the moment the way big sisters often did. "So what if you married Cruz and you adopted the kids together and he stayed here and you raised them while running your new school?"

"Give the lady a prize," Rory muttered as she slid onto the bench facing Kimberly. "That would be the first choice, of course, but since that's unlikely to happen, I think those sweet darlings are fated to be raised in Manhattan."

"It's a beautiful city with amazing facilities. They'll be fine." Kimberly yawned, then stretched her hand to Rory's. "But I'm sorry there isn't going to be a wedding. I would have taken great joy in getting everything ready for you. Sweet, simple and rooted in faith, the kind of wedding you've always wanted."

Rory shrugged. "In God's time, right? And in light of my crushing failure in the romance department, iced tea isn't cutting it. I need the real deal. Do you want a cone from Stan's?"

Enthusiasm lit Kimberly's eyes. "Not a cone. I want a banana split, the triple-scoop size. And I'm buying." She reached into her pocket and pulled out a twenty. "You go get them while I listen for Davy, and we can sit on the porch, eat our custards and remember all of our summers."

"Deal." She crossed The Square and brought the

sundaes back home a few minutes later. They sat on the porch, talking softly, long after they'd finished their sundaes. By the time Drew pulled up with Amy, little Dave was starting to fuss. The calm was broken, but it had been nice to share that time with Kimberly, especially when she wasn't in bossy big-sister mode. She reached out and gave Rory a hug while Drew changed the baby. "I never used to believe in God's timing."

Rory knew the truth in that. Her big sister had come to town pretty sure she could handle everything completely on her own. "I remember."

Kimberly smiled. "And then out of all the crazy, things started working out amazingly well."

Rory hugged her. "I love that you're still smart. Motherhood hasn't stolen all your brain cells."

"I love you, Rory."

"I know." Rory tipped her gaze up to Kimberly's. "Feeling's mutual. And I really like the kid, by the way," she added as Drew brought the baby their way. "Just looking at him makes me see everything a little brighter. A little better."

"Me, too."

The phone rang as Kimberly and Drew left. Holbrook School District was on the other end, asking to schedule an interview the next morning.

And there it was, the writing on the wall. Maybe she was meant to get this job. Maybe when the door closed on the Belker house, and nothing else became available, this was the window, sliding open.

"Yes, I can be there at nine thirty, and thank you." She hung up the phone with mixed emotion.

So many people would jump at the chance to be part of the guaranteed paycheck in the public school system. Benefits, retirement. Oh, she'd heard it all, for years.

And if that was what she was meant to do, she'd do it. It was a wonderful opportunity, a great chance to be gainfully employed and independent. If it meant putting her plans on hold, or putting them aside forever, perhaps that's what had to happen. If her dream of a school was supposed to become reality, wouldn't things have worked out sometime in the past two years?

Creeping shadows cooled the evening. Pots of flowers meant for Rosa's grave lined the walk. It had been too rainy to place them the week before, but the ground had dried.

She grabbed a small rake and shovel, a bag of mulch, some gardening gloves and the six potted plants. She drove the two miles to the cemetery, and made three trips across the section to carry everything to the grassy plot.

Rosa had ordered a small stone the year before, to mark Elina's and Maria's lives. It sat off to the right, next to Cruz's father's.

Rory turned the soft earth, shook out grass and weeds and gave the potted flowers a permanent home. She watered them from the pump-handled spigot along the cemetery path, then spread the mulch.

The site looked more peaceful now. Loved.

Soon there would be no direct family around to take care of the plot. But maybe Javi and Lily would come back someday, and when they did, they might visit their mother's stone, the family plot, and Rory wanted it to look loved.

She finished the job and packed up her things, and as she started the car, she looked back.

Rosa had made mistakes. Everyone did. But the one thing she'd taught her son was to go the distance. To do his best in everything.

As she looked at the small cheerful garden, she reconsidered tomorrow morning's interview.

If she was meant to be a regular teacher, would God have put this fire in her heart for the disadvantaged? No.

And if they offered her the position, would it be right to take it when someone else—someone more invested in that kind of teaching position—might appreciate it more and do it better?

It wouldn't be right. She'd be compounding the kind of mistake she abhorred, thinking of trading service solely because of money. And yet, she'd found out the hard way that starting a school was a costly process.

Gallaghers never give up.

Her grandma always said that, and her family proved it. They'd be fine with whatever decision she made, but the truth was, Rory wouldn't be fine with it.

She called Holbrook first thing the next morning, canceled the interview and had them remove her name from their list.

Yes, she loved teaching, but she had a dream, and she wasn't ready to give it up. Not yet.

She'd stay on the active substitute teacher list, and search for funding and a spot because, yes, a door might have closed a few weeks back—but that didn't mean the right window wasn't going to open. It merely meant she needed more patience and focus to see that it did.

Chapter Fifteen

Cruz looked around the newly divided office space overlooking The Square, then faced Chen Motsuma. "Are you all right taking lead in the office until school starts in two weeks?"

Chen crossed the new office. He tipped a blind and looked out the window. "A somewhat different view, Cruz."

Church spires rose between The Square and Canandaigua Lake beyond. "That's for sure. Do you think Lara and the kids will enjoy living here?"

He held up his phone. "Lara has already put our names on a church list, a school list and some kind of welcome thing from Gabby somebody or other."

"Gabby Gallagher, one of the best bakers around. That's a welcome basket you'll be happy to have land at your door."

"We've got the house pretty well set, and Lara's taking the kids on nature hikes every day. I think she's crazy glad I came to my senses, and now that Rodney lifted the lock on my funds…"

"The threatened lawsuit probably didn't hurt," Cruz acknowledged.

"It definitely tipped the scales in my favor." Chen motioned south toward Casa Blanca. "You get those other things done, get the little ones situated and, yes, I'll take charge here. And, Cruz," he added as Cruz started to move toward the door leading to Main Street. "Thank you."

Cruz gave him a thumbs-up. "We should have thought of this a long time ago. It's a shame it took family loss to give us a reason to change things, but I couldn't be starting this new enterprise with anyone better, Chen."

"Agreed."

Cruz walked outside, started to approach his car, then crossed The Square instead. He strolled over to Creighton Landing, knocked on the Gallagher door, and when Rory answered, he had to make his heart slow down so he could breathe half-right again. "Hey."

She looked up at him, then beyond him. "Hey."

He read the look. "The kids are at the house, helping Regina's daughter get stuff done. Which means they're most likely getting in the way."

"Packing is never fun."

"Why would they be packing?"

"For New York."

A ripple of anticipation rode up his spine because she hadn't heard about his change of plans, a fact that was directly related to her father being a non-talker. "Oh, yes. New York. About that…"

She didn't wait for him to finish. "Would it be okay if I come to visit them sometime? I know they were only with me for a few weeks, but I've actually known them since they first came to town, and I'd like the chance to see them. If that's okay," she added again. "I don't want to be disruptive, Cruz."

"I'd like that. In fact—" He leaned forward slightly, just close enough to appreciate the green and gold highlights in her caramel-toned eyes. "I'd love for you to visit, Rory. Anytime."

"You would?"

"Oh, yes." He smiled into the prettiest pair of surprised eyes he'd ever seen. "Got time for a cone?"

"A cone?" She glanced from him to Stan's Custard Stand and back, and when a slight smile teased her lips, Cruz figured he might be making some progress. "I'd be a fool to say no."

He tipped his head toward Stan's and held out a hand. "Summer will be over soon. No one should waste a chance to get custard on a perfect August day."

"No, they shouldn't." She put her hand in his.

He closed his fingers around hers and it felt so right that he almost said too much. He stopped himself, but it wasn't easy. A custard cone first.

And the hand-holding was nice, too.

And then maybe she'd come out to the house, and see what he'd been doing since packing hadn't entered into the equation.

They walked up to Stan's window, still hand in hand. "Cone? Dish? Sundae?"

"A cone," she decided, scanning Stan's list. "A waffle cone with Dynamite Crunch."

He checked out the display, then held up two fingers. "Make that two." And when they had their cones, he didn't suggest they sit. He took her hand again, and led her toward the water.

"You're not working today?" She eyed their hands,

the cones and the town clock snugged along the edge of The Square.

"I took a few days off to get things in order. We weren't done with fix-up projects when Mom passed away, so those had to be completed. And I had a few odd things to take care of. Your dad jumped in on those. He's been a big help."

"He's a wonderful man. I'm not surprised you like him."

He bumped shoulders with her. "Because I'm pretty nice, too?"

She started to say something, and he paused, stopped and faced her, just before they reached the thick ribbon of sand. "I want to apologize for not telling you about the Belker place sooner. I felt bad that I'd done it when you told me about your dream, but I should have told you right away. I'm sorry, Rory. I promise I won't be keeping any more secrets from you. Okay? Will you forgive me?" He tipped his gaze down to her. "How I wish you would."

He wouldn't be keeping secrets from her?

As in...in the future he wouldn't keep secrets from her? But they didn't have a future.

Did they?

She licked her cone to avoid it dripping down the front of her shirt, then answered, "I was too sensitive."

When he started to argue, she said, "Shush."

He shushed. And smiled.

"I thought about it after I got upset, and I realized that you were only doing what you're supposed to do. You see a great deal, you seize it. I do the same thing at the mall, but with fewer zeroes after the dollar signs.

I shouldn't have blamed you for being good at what you do. I was mad that I got bested and I overreacted. My bad."

"So you're sorry?"

"I do believe I suggested that."

He slanted her a quizzical look. "And yet you didn't say it outright."

"I have to say it outright?"

He grinned, waiting.

She puffed out a long breath of air. "I'm sorry, Cruz."

"Your cone's dripping."

It was, and it took a minute to regain the upper hand with her cone. By the time she did, they'd reached the sand. "I love it here," he mused as they walked along the edge. Not too many people were sitting along the beach, but dozens were swimming, sunbathing and water-skiing. "I'd forgotten how beautiful it really is."

"You could always keep the house and use it for vacations," she suggested. "Although it's a pricey property to use that way. Or get something smaller when you sell, and that way the kids can have time up here as they grow. I think those memories would go a long way toward healing old hurts in little lives."

"It's a thought." He glanced at his watch and his eyebrows shot up. "And I've got to get back home. Regina's daughter has an appointment tonight, and I don't want to make her late. Are you working tomorrow?"

She flushed because the answer to that was a flat-out no. "Not until they call for subbing jobs once school starts."

"Great." He paused, looped their joined hands around her back and faced her. "Can you drive up to Casa Blanca tomorrow morning? The kids would love to see you."

He didn't add that they needed to say their good-byes. He didn't have to add it, because as the calendar days marched on, September loomed with all the sensibility of scheduling that fall required. "I can do that."

"Good." He held her hand like that, their arms looped around her, and if he wanted to pull her closer, he could.

He didn't. He brought her arm back around and finished his cone as they walked up her driveway. "Thanks for walking with me."

"Thanks for the custard."

He touched a finger to the brim of that old baseball cap. "My pleasure."

He crossed The Square, got into his car, merged with busy commuter traffic and disappeared to the south.

She sank onto the garden bench, wondering.

He'd flirted with her. Held her hand. Invited her over.

Why?

Did his heart jump rhythm like hers did whenever he was around? Or was he just being a really nice guy to the woman who'd helped teach his children?

She wasn't sure, but she knew one thing: whatever he was doing, she liked it.

Tyler, Badge and Jim had delivered three expectant nanny goats to the newly fenced and cleaned goat barn the previous morning. Just seeing those three lovely ladies climbing the staged rocks and tree stumps made Cruz smile.

What if she says no? What if she tells you and your inflated ego to take a hike?

Life was full of chances. So was romance. But Rory sure did seem to like walking and talking.

Maybe it was the stuffed waffle cone. He was willing to admit it was really good custard.

But maybe it wasn't just the frozen treat, or the walk along the sandy beach. Maybe—just maybe— it was him.

Rory pulled into the newly sealed front lot the next morning. The place looked good. So good. Fresh and white, the expansive house stood in stately fashion, full of charm. The grounds were golf-course pretty, with the grass cut, green and smooth. The whole place looked beautiful, like she remembered from so long ago.

She smiled and bent low when the kids raced toward her. "Hey, darlings, how are you? I've missed you so much!"

"Cruz got us a s'prise!"

"But we're not supposed to tell," added Lily. She scolded Javier with her hands on her hips, total Rosa. "Cruz said we needed to wait. Did you forget?"

"Sowry!"

"Hey, you got the *r* sound in that one!" She high-fived the little guy and hugged him. "Well done, my friend! And remember what we learned about good secrets?"

Javier put a finger to his mouth. "Shh."

"Yes, so don't say another thing about it, okay?"

"'Cept it's hard because it's such a good s'prise!"

She stood back up. Cruz was eyeing the kids with a rueful look and he rubbed his chin the way he did when he was musing something. "Remind me to never discuss business dealings with them around, okay?"

"I'll send regular memos to Manhattan."

He nodded. "Perfect. Hey, these guys wanted to take a walk along the creek, and I figured our time is going to wind down soon. Care to go with us?"

Two adorable kids grabbed her hands. "Please, Rory!"

"Yes, pwease?" Javier tipped those big brown eyes her way. "You never do fun stuff wif all of us anymore, and I miss you so much."

"So do I."

Cruz didn't just say that, did he? One quick glance his way confirmed it.

She took Javier's hand on one side and Lily's on the other. "Lead the way, darlings."

"Fank you!" Such a simple thing to make a little guy so happy. They walked to the low-level creek and strolled along the grassy knoll just above the water.

"I found fwee fwogs yesterday." Javi held tight to her hand and peered over, into the water. "They were right there!" He pointed and almost upended them both into the creek.

"Whoa." Cruz snugged an arm around her.

It felt good and right to be there, in the safety of Cruz's arm, the scent of spicy soap and morning coffee a delightful combination. If she turned, just so, she'd be face-to-face with him, kissably close.

But why tempt fate?

She took a step back from the edge, drawing Javi with her. "Let's avoid getting wet this morning, okay? I didn't bring any extra clothes with me."

"Cruz! Can we go show Rory our new friends?"

"Which ones?"

"You have a bunch of new friends?" She tipped Lily's chin up and made a skeptical face. "How can this be, my little gingersnap?"

A noise sounded just then. A blatting noise, from back toward the barns behind them. "What was that?"

Cruz put up his hands as if warding off the question.

Lily and Javi turned around and tugged her back toward the farm. "Some of our new friends, Miss Rory! You are going to love them so much!"

"One is gway, one is white and one is so many colors!" Javi leaned closer and lowered his voice. "I fink she's the pwettiest one of all."

They turned the corner from the creek, facing the lower barn. New fencing ran along the small pasture's edge, and three rounded goats blinked a welcome from the other side of the fence.

Rory blinked right back.

"I told you we had a s'prise!" Javier pumped her hand. "Cwuz got them for us because he said goat milk was good for kids and candy."

"He said that?" This wasn't making sense…unless…

He met her look of surprise and nodded. "My mother had a thing for goat's milk. It seemed fitting to bring a few ladies back on board."

"But—"

"They're pretty, right?"

She laughed because having Cruz call goats pretty seemed out of character and delightful. "Lovely, actually. Do they have names?"

"We helped Cruz name them!" Lily wrung her hand, excited. "Guess what their names are?"

"Out of thin air? Out of the millions of possibilities? You want me to come up with random names?"

Cruz leaned close. "Think royal females familiar to small children." He stressed the word *royal* and winked.

Princesses.

She smiled up at him, then pointed. "Belle."

"How did you know?" Lily stared at her, dumbfounded.

"Because you love *Beauty and the Beast*," Rory replied. "And Elsa."

"Nope."

"Anna."

"Yes!" Lily and Javier both laughed. "But you don't know the third one, and I don't think you'll guess it," Lily decided. "She's different."

Cruz pinched his thumb and forefinger together in a silent clue. *A tiny princess...*

"Tinkerbell."

"I can't believe you got it!" Lily grabbed hold of her and spun her around. "Rory, you are the smartest person about princesses I know!"

"Well, we all have our gifts, I suppose." She couldn't avoid a wry tone, because there probably should be more important gifts than naming fairy-tale heroines, but if it made a beautiful child happy, she was okay with that. "I think this is one of the coolest surprises ever, guys."

"But we have another one, too," Javi exclaimed, then clapped his hands over his mouth. He couldn't stay quiet, so he whispered around the little fingers. "It's a very cool s'pwise!"

"It is," Cruz admitted. "I think it's even better than the goats myself."

"Better than goats?" Rory smiled up at him and nudged him with her elbow. "What could be better than goats? And who's going to take care of the goats when you're away?"

"Cwuz!" Javi jumped on him. "Are you going away?"

"Nope. I'm not, little man, I'm staying right here with you." He held Javi snug in his left arm. "And did you forget what I said?" He bumped foreheads with Javi until their eyelashes touched. "Shh."

Javi giggled, then pushed his face into Cruz's neck, laughing.

It was a beautiful sight, man and boy, connecting in the very same spot that Cruz had run and played as a child. He noticed her approval, then bumped her shoulder with his. "You like the goats?"

She reached out and ran a hand across Tinkerbell's head. "I love the goats. They're perfect. And they seem quite at home."

"I thought so, too."

"And I think I've seen these goats before, when they were younger ladies. At Tyler's farm?"

"You've got a good eye for goats."

"That, and he's the only one nearby raising dairy goats. Gosh, they're darlings. Three pretty goats."

"And their babies," Lily explained. "So six little goats. Or more, if they have twins!"

"Good point. So that's a bit different, isn't it?"

Cruz put a hand beneath her arm as they moved up the hill. "Busy, but good. I have it on good authority that being busy is in children's best interests."

It was, of course, but the children would be hours away. Not exactly available for goat care.

A car pulled into the half-circle drive. It parked and Clint Jackson got out and came their way, looking like a man on a mission. Clint's construction crew handled jobs ranging from remodeling old homes to building new neighborhoods. His firm had been the general contractor on Kimberly and Drew's new house. "Cruz." He shook Cruz's hand and smiled at Rory. "Rory, hey. How's it going?"

"Well, thank you. Good to see you. I know you've been busy with those new developments just out of town. Kimberly and Drew love their house, Clint."

"Dad and I are glad of the business, that's for sure. Cruz, are you ready to see the ideas I worked up?"

Cruz nodded as Rory edged away. "I can keep the kids busy and leave you to this."

"Actually I'd like to run these ideas by you. That's why I had Clint come by now."

"You're doing something for the kids?"

Clint let Rory precede him into the sprawling house. He turned right and moved toward the bigger party room, farthest from the living side of the house. "Kid-oriented, yes. Rory, I'm not a father, and I don't know a ton about little kids, so your advice is crucial."

"I'll do what I can, of course."

The kids had come inside with them, but when Regina's daughter called them for freeze pops, they dashed that way.

Cruz moved up behind her, close enough so if she moved, they'd touch, which meant she didn't dare move.

Clint moved to a table and unrolled the plans. He

pointed to the wall just inside the door. "I was thinking of a cubby wall here. A work area here, with space to move because this room is huge. Prayer circle/reading circle here, and that extends into the open play area that's fed with natural light all year long, even on the gloomiest and shortest days of winter. And because this room is huge, I thought we'd turn it into two rooms, and do a mirror image on this side."

"Two rooms? For two kids? Couldn't the front room become a den or a study or something? That would make more sense."

"You make a good point." Cruz stayed silent for long ticks of the grandfather clock counting time in the extended foyer behind them. "But what if it wasn't just two kids?" He leaned closer and lowered his mouth close to her ear, so close that his breath tickled her cheek. "What if it was more like a dozen kids or so, in each room. Coming to school here, morning and afternoon?"

"Coming to school?" She looked at him, because he couldn't possibly mean...

Close. So close. His dark eyes and thick brows, and the much darker hue of his skin tone after working the vineyards with her father.

He smiled at her. Right at her. Then he indicated the plans in front of them. "See, I heard there was this amazing woman, a teacher, looking for funding for a preschool to help kids get a great start in school and life. I was told she needed a place to set up this school, and I happen to have this big beautiful space just sitting here. It would be a shame to let it go to waste, wouldn't it?"

Oh, what an opportunity.

A site, a permanent site, just what she'd hoped for. Set on a verdant hill, surrounded by beauty on all sides, and with access and parking for parents. But how hard would it be to come to Casa Blanca every day, thinking of Cruz and the kids and what could have been?

You talk about sacrifice all the time. Maybe this is meant to be yours. This isn't just a good offer, it's a great offer.

She knew that. But she also knew that most things came with a price tag attached. "How much are we talking in rent?"

"Negotiable."

She shook her head quickly. "You're a lawyer. You know it's not in my best interests to enter a business deal without agreed contract stipulations."

"Good point. So maybe we could agree on them right now."

"I'm listening."

Clint eased away while they faced off, which was probably a smart move on his part.

Cruz pointed to the beautifully appointed room. "I offer you free lifetime use of the room in exchange for making me the happiest man in the world."

What?

She frowned, but as he dropped down to one knee, her heart did a flip and her palms grew moist. "Cruz."

"Rory Gallagher, I've had enough of the big city, and my work can be done from most anywhere, so I've decided I'd like to do it here. I'd like to stay in Grace Haven, marry the most wonderful woman on earth and raise cute kids with you. If you'll have me, that is."

Have him? Was he serious? She locked eyes with him. "The school room is part of the deal?"

He nodded.

"And no rent?"

He laughed. "None. But I will use it as a tax write-off against your business."

She put one hand on either side of his face, leaned down and kissed him, slow and sweet. And when she was done kissing him, she tilted her head as if still considering. "You drive a hard bargain."

"I've been told that before." He was still smiling.

"But you kiss really well."

"On that I plead the Fifth," he told her, and stood. He wrapped her in his arms and held her gaze. "So what do you think, Rory? Will you marry me and run your school here and be my wife forever?"

She kissed him one more time. "I most certainly will."

"Perfect." He kissed her back, long, slow and sweet, and then gathered her into the hug she'd been missing these past few weeks. "Shall we tell the kids?"

She drew back and pointed toward the kitchen, where two little faces peeked around the corner. "I think they figured it out."

The kids giggled out loud, then raced their way.

Rory tipped her head back and gazed up at him. "You're really okay with staying here?"

"I'm opening an office opposite The Square with one of my colleagues, and that's exactly where I want to be, honey. From this day forward I want to be at home in Grace Haven with you. And them." He winked as the kids tackled into them. "And I'm pretty sure there won't be a dull moment for the rest of our lives."

"Which only makes it better." She reached up and

pulled him down for one last kiss before hugging the kids. "Welcome home, Cruz."

His smile said the words made him happy. "Glad to be here."

Epilogue

A vineyard wedding.

His vineyard wedding.

Cruz refused to be the least bit nervous, but as people began filling the white-draped chairs on either side of the stone walk, his hands went damp.

A few months ago he'd driven upstate in a total funk. He hadn't wanted to return, face his mother or fix someone else's mistakes.

Somewhere along the way he'd grown a heart, or maybe found one he'd had all along.

The music started. Chen moved up alongside, to stand with him. Chen's wife and two kids were in the second row, surrounded by New York friends and families.

Badge, Tyler and Jim were there, too, and they looked pretty proud. Sadie and her husband were sitting beside them, and old Miss Belker sat to their right. When Tinkerbell and Anna began bleating in the lower pasture, the three old-timers grinned and high-fived one another.

The chairs were full of people from town, the voluminous Gallagher family, neighbors, several of his mother's friends from the Mennonite community and a few New York dignitaries.

All of that faded into the background when Rory stepped into the yard.

Javi came forward, carrying rings. He tried to walk slowly, like they'd practiced, but the minute he spotted Cruz, his feet sped up.

Lily followed in a pretty pink dress, sprinkling colorful rose petals along the path, winning hearts as she strolled forward.

Emily and Kimberly followed, and then his bride.

His bride.

Pete escorted her along the walk as the congregation stood to welcome her.

Beautiful.

She'd left her hair down, for him. She didn't wear a veil, but a tiny crown of handwoven rosebuds and greens circled her head.

And as her father brought her closer, she smiled at Cruz. Just at Cruz.

He reached out, took her hand and broke every rule by feathering the lightest of kisses to her lips. "Nice to see you."

She smiled up at him. "You, too."

"Great dress."

Her smile went wider. "Glad you like it." She indicated where Steve stood, waiting. "You ready to do this?"

Cruz was more than ready. "It feels like I've been waiting all my life to do this," he told her, smiling.

She squeezed his hand lightly. "Then let's go."

She turned toward Steve. So did Cruz. And when

her uncle began the beautiful, classic ceremony, it felt
like everything had come together perfectly.

At long last.

* * * * *

*If you loved this story, pick up the other books
in the GRACE HAVEN series:*

*AN UNEXPECTED GROOM
HER UNEXPECTED FAMILY*

*And check out these other stories of small-town life
from author Ruth Logan Herne's previous
miniseries KIRKWOOD LAKE:*

*THE LAWMAN'S HOLIDAY WISH
LOVING THE LAWMAN
HER HOLIDAY FAMILY
HEALING THE LAWMAN'S HEART*

Available now from Love Inspired!

Find more great reads at www.LoveInspired.com

Dear Reader,

I absolutely loved writing this beautiful story for multiple reasons. I live in upstate New York, an area ripe with farm produce, orchards, vineyards and seasonal workers. We have local programs to help the children of farm workers, but when the economy takes a hit, programs sometimes get labeled "nonessential." I not only raised six kids, I've helped raise dozens of others, and getting kids off to a good start is vital. Enter Rory, wanting to use her education to make a difference for kids from low-income or disadvantaged families. But rules don't allow us to simply plant schools here and there.

Cruz comes back to town carrying a load of bitterness. So much of his family history is unresolved. But when the fate of two small children cracks his facade, he begins to see a new light.

God works in amazing ways. I don't just believe that, I see it daily. Watching Cruz and Rosa find common ground after their long estrangement made me hopeful that families can come to see that peace on earth begins right here, with us, with our families. Mother Teresa often said, "Peace begins with a smile." Let's prove that today!

I love to hear from readers. You can reach me through my website, ruthloganherne.com, or come friend me on Facebook at Ruth Logan Herne. I love to chat, play and pray with friends there! I'm also one of the cooks at the Yankee Belle Café, which you can visit online at yankeebellecafe.blogspot.com. You can email me at loganherne@gmail.com or snail mail me through the great folks at Love Inspired, 24th Floor, 195 Broadway, New York, NY 10007.

And once again, thank you so much for taking the time to read this beautiful story.

God bless you!
Ruthy

COMING NEXT MONTH FROM
Love Inspired®

Available May 23, 2017

THEIR PRETEND AMISH COURTSHIP
The Amish Bachelors • by Patricia Davids

To avoid their matchmaking mothers' plans and pursue their dreams, Fannie Erb and Noah Bowman agree to a pretend courtship. As they make room in their schedules to attend events as a couple, could their hearts also begin to make room for each other?

LONE STAR BACHELOR
The Buchanons • by Linda Goodnight

Content with his bachelor life, builder Sawyer Buchanon's world is turned upside down when he meets pretty PI Jade Warren. Jade was raised to never trust a Buchanon, but when she's hired to investigate the vandalism at Sawyer's building projects, the Texas charmer soon sweeps her off her feet.

SECOND-CHANCE COWBOY
Cowboys of Cedar Ridge • by Carolyne Aarsen

Once she's paid off her father's debts, Tabitha Rennie plans to leave Cedar Ridge and all the painful memories it brings. Having ex-fiancé Morgan Walsh ask for help connecting with his son was not part of the plan. Yet spending time with father and son is creating dreams of house and home.

FALLING FOR THE RANCHER
Aspen Creek Crossroads • by Roxanne Rustand

As a single mom, veterinarian Darcy Leighton would do anything for her daughter—including remaining at the clinic with rancher vet Logan Maxwell, the man who bought the place out from under her. As they work together, their truce turns to friendship—and to the discovery of a once-in-a-lifetime love.

THE SINGLE MOM'S SECOND CHANCE
Goose Harbor • by Jessica Keller

Returning to Goose Harbor, Claire Atwood has plenty of reasons for staying away from Evan Daniels—most notably being jilted at the altar by her onetime sweetheart. But both are running for mayor, which means spending time together. But could it also mean a second chance at forever?

HOMETOWN HERO'S REDEMPTION
by Jill Kemerer

When rugged firefighter Drew Gannon asks her to babysit troubled ten-year-old Wyatt, Lauren Pierce can't help but recall their high school rivalry. Can the temporary single dad prove to the pretty former social worker he's no longer the foolhardy teen she once knew—and he's actually her perfect match?

LOOK FOR THESE AND OTHER LOVE INSPIRED BOOKS WHEREVER BOOKS ARE SOLD, INCLUDING MOST BOOKSTORES, SUPERMARKETS, DISCOUNT STORES AND DRUGSTORES.

LICNM0517

Get 2 Free Books,

Plus 2 Free Gifts—
just for trying the Reader Service!

Love Inspired®

YES! Please send me 2 FREE Love Inspired® Romance novels and my 2 FREE mystery gifts (gifts are worth about $10 retail). After receiving them, if I don't wish to receive any more books, I can return the shipping statement marked "cancel." If I don't cancel, I will receive 6 brand-new novels every month and be billed just $5.24 for the regular-print edition or $5.74 each for the larger-print edition in the U.S., or $5.74 each for the regular-print edition or $6.24 each for the larger-print edition in Canada. That's a saving of at least 13% off the cover price. It's quite a bargain! Shipping and handling is just 50¢ per book in the U.S. and 75¢ per book in Canada.* I understand that accepting the 2 free books and gifts places me under no obligation to buy anything. I can always return a shipment and cancel at any time. Even if I never buy another book, the 2 free books and gifts are mine to keep forever.

Please check one:
☐ Love Inspired Romance Regular-Print   ☐ Love Inspired Romance Larger-Print
  (105/305 IDN GLQC)   (122/322 IDN GLQD)

Name _____ (PLEASE PRINT) _____

Address _____ Apt. # _____

City _____ State/Province _____ Zip/Postal Code _____

Signature (if under 18, a parent or guardian must sign) _____

Mail to the **Reader Service:**
IN U.S.A.: P.O. Box 1867, Buffalo, NY 14240-1867
IN CANADA: P.O. Box 611, Fort Erie, Ontario L2A 9Z9

Want to try two free books from another line?
Call 1-800-873-8635 today or visit www.ReaderService.com.

*Terms and prices subject to change without notice. Prices do not include applicable taxes. Sales tax applicable in N.Y. Canadian residents will be charged applicable taxes. Offer not valid in Quebec. This offer is limited to one order per household. Books received may not be as shown. Not valid for current subscribers to Love Inspired Romance books. All orders subject to credit approval. Credit or debit balances in a customer's account(s) may be offset by any other outstanding balance owed by or to the customer. Please allow 4 to 6 weeks for delivery. Offer available while quantities last.

Your Privacy—The Reader Service is committed to protecting your privacy. Our Privacy Policy is available online at www.ReaderService.com or upon request from the Reader Service.

We make a portion of our mailing list available to reputable third parties that offer products we believe may interest you. If you prefer that we not exchange your name with third parties, or if you wish to clarify or modify your communication preferences, please visit us at www.ReaderService.com/consumerschoice or write to us at Reader Service Preference Service, P.O. Box 9062, Buffalo, NY 14240-9062. Include your complete name and address.

LI17R

SPECIAL EXCERPT FROM

Love Inspired

*Will a pretend courtship fend off matchmaking mothers,
or will it lead to true love?*

*Read on for a sneak preview of
THEIR PRETEND AMISH COURTSHIP,
the next book in* **Patricia Davids**'s
heartwarming series, **AMISH BACHELORS**.

"Noah, where are you? I need to speak to you."

Working near the back of his father's barn, Noah
Bowman dropped the hoof of his buggy horse Willy, took
the last nail out of his mouth and stood upright to stare
over his horse's back. Fannie Erb, his neighbor's youngest
daughter, came hurrying down the wide center aisle,
checking each stall as she passed. Her white *kapp* hung
off the back of her head dangling by a single bobby pin.
Her curly red hair was still in a bun, but it was windblown
and lopsided. No doubt, it would be completely undone
before she got home. Fannie was always in a rush.

"What's up, *karotte oben*?" He picked up his horse's
hoof again, positioned it between his knees and drove in
the last nail of the new shoe.

Fannie stopped outside the stall gate and fisted her
hands on her hips. "You know I hate being called a carrot
top."

"Sorry." Noah grinned.

He wasn't sorry a bit. He liked the way her unusual violet eyes darkened and flashed when she was annoyed. Annoying Fannie had been one of his favorite pastimes when they were schoolchildren.

Framed as she was in a rectangle of light cast by the early-morning sun shining through the open top of a Dutch door, dust motes danced around Fannie's head like fireflies drawn to the fire in her hair. The summer sun had expanded the freckles on her upturned nose and given her skin a healthy glow, but Fannie didn't tan the way most women did. Her skin always looked cool and creamy. As usual, she was wearing blue jeans and riding boots under her plain green dress and black apron.

"What you need, Fannie? Did your hot temper spark a fire and you want me to put it out?" He chuckled at his own wit. He along with his four brothers were volunteer members of the local fire department.

"This isn't a joke, Noah. I need to get engaged, and quickly. Will you help me?"

Don't miss
THEIR PRETEND AMISH COURTSHIP
by Patricia Davids, available June 2017 wherever
Love Inspired® books and ebooks are sold.

www.LoveInspired.com

Copyright © 2017 by Patricia MacDonald

LIEXP0517

EXCLUSIVE LIMITED TIME OFFER AT
www.HARLEQUIN.com

SECRETS HIDDEN AMONG
THE MAGNOLIA TREES

The
INNKEEPER'S
Sister

NEW YORK TIMES BESTSELLING AUTHOR

LINDA
GOODNIGHT

$15.99 U.S./$18.99 CAN.

$1.⁵⁰ OFF

New York Times Bestselling Author

LINDA
GOODNIGHT

welcomes you to Honey Ridge,
Tennessee, where long-buried secrets
lead to some startling realizations in

The INNKEEPER'S
Sister

Available April 25, 2017
Get your copy today!

Receive $1.50 OFF the purchase price of
THE INNKEEPER'S SISTER by Linda Goodnight
when you use the coupon code below on Harlequin.com

SISTERS17

Offer valid from April 25, 2017, until May 31, 2017, on www.Harlequin.com.

Valid in the U.S.A. and Canada only. To redeem this offer, please add the print
or ebook version of THE INNKEEPER'S SISTER by Linda Goodnight to your
shopping cart and then enter the coupon code at checkout.

DISCLAIMER: Offer valid on the print or ebook version of THE INNKEEPER'S
SISTER by Linda Goodnight from April 25, 2017, at 12:01 a.m. ET until
May 31, 2017, 11:59 p.m. ET at www.Harlequin.com only. The Customer will
receive $1.50 OFF the list price of THE INNKEEPER'S SISTER by Linda Goodnight
in print or ebook on www.Harlequin.com with the SISTERS17 coupon code.
Sales tax applied where applicable. Quantities are limited. Valid in the U.S.A. and
Canada only. All orders subject to approval.

HQN™

www.HQNBooks.com

® and ™ are trademarks owned and used by the trademark owner and/or its licensee.
© 2017 Harlequin Enterprises Limited

PHCOUPLGLI0517

Turn your love of reading into rewards you'll love with
Harlequin My Rewards

Join for FREE today at
www.HarlequinMyRewards.com

Earn **FREE BOOKS** of your choice.

Experience **EXCLUSIVE OFFERS** and contests.

Enjoy **BOOK RECOMMENDATIONS** selected just for you.

PLUS! Sign up now and get **500** points right away!

Earn **FREE** REWARDS
HarlequinMyRewards.com
Join Today!

MYR16R